Love Lingers Still: A Haunted Anthology of Lost Loved Ones

Edited by Marinda K Dennis

Published by Energy Threads, LLC
Nebraska, U.S.A.
www.Energy-Threads.com

Love Lingers Still

Manuscript to book by Marinda K Dennis
Cover Art by Adelita Chavoya

The tales within this work are all works of fiction and creative non-fiction. All characters, products, corporations, institutions, and/or entities of any kind in this book are either products of the authors' imaginations OR, if real, used creatively without intent to describe actual characteristics or have had the names changed to protect the identities of those referenced. All pieces are a reflection of the author's own workings and not that of Energy Threads.

First Energy Threads trade paperback printing, 2023

ISBN: 978-1-959879-00-8

DEDICATION

Every haunting, even those that are romanticized, has one horrifying, underlying truth: someone we once loved is no longer with us. It could be a parent, a spouse, a friend, or even a child who haunts our most heartfelt memories. This anthology is born of just such a pain. My teenage daughter Angel lost her father, her father's favorite grandmother, and then her own favorite great-grandmother. She was pained with each new loss, but the last struck her the deepest. We believe that on some level it was the last that lead her to take her own life at the tender age of fifteen.

This anthology is dedicated to the lost loved ones of the contributing authors, to my little Honeybee, and to all we have lost over the years. May the stories contained in these pages help those who are grieving a loss of their own. Remember that your loved ones walk with you even now. They watch over you and give you little signs to show you that their love lingers still.

This book is dedicated to all of the lost loved ones over the years. May their souls rest in peace as they watch over us from on   high.

CONTENTS

ACKNOWLEDGMENTS

A big thank you to everyone who contributed, author and artist alike, to make this book what it is. Without your art, your stories, and your belief in this project, there would not be an anthology to commemorate our dearly departed. My hope is that each of your pieces will inspire a wealth of healing. To a world filled with loss, we offer you this moment of solace, of catharsis, of sweet sorrow amid the pain of parting.

1. How to Say Goodbye to Fern
by Ellen Meister

1. Be there to answer the phone when her husband calls to say Fern has had enough and will be going home to take hospice care. Say "I understand" when he explains that it was her decision. Say it again when he tells you that if you are going to pray for her, please do not pray for her to get well. Pray for her to die quickly.

2. Light a candle and do as you are told. Ask God to take her quickly. Do not wish for a miracle.

3. When her husband calls again to say come now if you want to say good-bye, do not cry on the phone. Wait until you hang up. Then fall to your knees and wail in selfish abandon. She was your best friend. You are too young for her to die.

4. Say okay when your husband insists on going with you. Understand he wants to say good-bye, too. And also, he doesn't want you driving alone like this. He is afraid you are so distraught you will wrap the car around a tree, leaving him and

the children all alone. For a terrible moment, resent Fern for having the freedom to die without leaving anyone motherless.

5. Rest your face against the cool glass of the window and say nothing when your husband reaches over and squeezes your hand.

6. Try not to panic when you see other cars in front of her house, even though you thought you would have her to yourself.

7. Sit limply at her bedside with the others, smelling death. Notice that she is lucid, but her eyes are already dead. Be patient as you wait for someone to understand that you are her oldest friend and have the greatest claim. When no one speaks up, make the announcement yourself; ask them to leave you alone with her for a few minutes.

8. When she turns to you and says, "What do you want to ask me?" go blank. Tell her you just want her to know how much you love her. When she answers, "You were everything," let yourself weep and weep and weep.

9. Later, agree with your husband when he says it is silly to cancel the trip; she could hang on for weeks. But know in your heart that your cellphone will ring while you are in Disney World.

10. Then, when it happens, on a recklessly sunny day just as you are climbing into a ferryboat to Magic Kingdom, thank the caller for letting you know. You will be the only one crying on the boat, but soon you will stop. You have forever to mourn your friend. Today you will go to Pirates of the Caribbean.

2. The Funeral
By Quantre Moore

Growing up without a lot of friends and wanting to be left alone, I would tend to pay attention to the little things not everyone would notice. View it as you want. I saw it more as a curse. I had to grow up quicker than the other kids my age due to my own self isolation, constant let downs, and the hostile environment I called home. I had convinced myself that being alone was better than all emotions, whether they be positive or negative. I taught myself to believe that emotions were pointless, so I hid them along with my true inner child.

I couldn't have been any older than ten or eleven. It was a day unlike any other in the middle of summer. I was getting ready to attend a funeral, one for an old family friend and former teacher. For such an occasion I put on my Sunday best: a collared Polo, nice jeans, and the only jacket I felt safe in. My mom, my sister, and I drove to the venue. On the long ride, I felt as if I was boiling alive because I refused to take my jacket off no matter how many times I was told to do so. The car was filled with nothing but silence, the only sounds crept in from outside.

The funeral was held in a small community church. Cars wrapped around the building. Once inside, I looked around and saw some new faces, some old, but every last person had the same expression: grief, mourning the lost, holding nothing back. There were so many people collectively crying together that you could hear them from outside. You could clearly tell that the dearly departed was loved while they were alive. She had been part of a dance company and had a huge impact on all of these people's lives, those young and old.

All the seats were already occupied, so we stood in the back when the services started. As time went on, I felt my legs weaken. I swayed side to side in an attempt to stay standing. By the time I was ready to throw in the towel and sit, I heard someone singing. What I heard was the softest, most elegant voice. I suddenly felt like crying, but I didn't know why.

And yet, when I had seen this lovely woman lying in her coffin, the women whom I once thought of as family, someone I use to hold dear to my heart, someone who helped to raise me when I was young and taught me rhythm and how to dance… in that moment I felt nothing. It was not because anything bad happened between us. I realized that it was because as we both got older, I didn't think much about her due to the distance of time. Until eventually I had completely forgotten her.

Despite those repressed emotions, tears still tried to escape while the music welled up inside me. Choking them back I felt a huge lump in my throat suffocating me, but I held on not wanting to look weak. I glanced around the room and spotted my mom. I realized that even though I hadn't heard her, she had been crying this whole time.

The song came to an end, and people lined up to say their final good-byes before the burial. I walked up to the coffin, staring at a once familiar face that seemed foreign to me now. In the car I looked out the window in front. There was a long line of cars heading to the burial site. Amongst the original line there was the occasional random driver who would merge into the funeral procession line with us.

With emotions high, the streets filled with angry divers and horns blaring at one another. My mom almost in tears shouted, "Get out of line! Can't you see this is a funeral!?" Every passing second the noises grew louder and louder. To tune them out I cleared my mind of anything outside and turned inward to be me alone with my own thoughts.

Complete and utter silence was something of bliss: no distraction, no one to bother me, just me and me alone. We arrived at the graveyard to the site of miles of headstones of all shapes and sizes. We walked up to a hole in the ground where six men carried the wooden casket. Everyone tried to hold their composure as the pastor said his last words.

Gradually, people left one by one. When my mother eventually motioned that we too needed to go, I followed her. Something in me paused, and I took a glance back to the open grave. The last thing I saw was the casket being lowered. After that we left for home, and all I could think was "Is this truly how life ends: buried in an expensive box, six feet under with nothing but a tombstone, our names engraved on it to show we once existed?"

3. A Haunted House
By Gregory Norris

Silas was the cool uncle; the one who let Marie finger-paint on the hundred-year-old hardwood floor of the front parlor, telling her the smudges added to the room's ambience; who never forgot her birthday or Christmases even when her deadbeat father did; who left her the big house on Maple Street with its sunny front parlor, ancient lilac trees, and views all the way down to the river.

Uncle Silas did so with one caveat: "When I die, the house and everything inside are yours to do with as you want—apart from the front parlor. Do not change one detail, or I'll return to haunt you," he'd tease lightly, and, until the warning was tested, Marie always laughed, thinking the threat a joke.

After Uncle Silas died, they scattered his ashes around the yard, as he'd requested; and instead of a funeral, Marie threw a party. They played his favorite music, ate little finger sandwiches and pastries slathered in sunny yellow icing and decorated in fresh berries from the good bakery downtown, and told stories about a man who had lived a long and fulfilling life that were happy in their center and only sad around the edges. They toasted Silas in cups of Earl Grey tea, his favorite.

"To the coolest uncle ever," Marie said.

He left her the house, a sizeable insurance policy, and money in the bank. Silas had kept all of the bills paid right up to his departure, meaning Marie would be well off and able to pursue her own dreams as a result.

In the days and nights that followed the party, she searched the house for any sign of his ghost but found none. Uncle Silas was gone.

The front parlor was a grand room with classic furniture detailed in so many carved wings and claws that she often imagined the sofa and chairs either running away or taking flight, with bay windows that received plenty of daylight. It also served as a gallery of mostly unfamiliar faces. Dozens of strangers stared down from frames on walls, few of which Marie recognized. Oh, she knew their stories—over the years, Silas had pointed out the grandmothers Marie never met, the great grandparents, and a host of uncles, aunts, and long-deceased cats, all lovingly beatified within the halos of gold-gilt frames and some with elaborate wedding cake rosettes.

The floor still showed blotches of paint from past art lessons. *Strange*, Marie thought on that day, that he never cleaned up her messes, until she remembered that the oversight was intentional—one more tribute to family in a room filled with so much brightness that it was easy to overlook that the front parlor was a kind of sepulcher.

She attempted to read, do needlepoint, and play games on her phone or tablet in that room, only too many eyes stared at her without blinking; and Marie found herself avoiding what had always been the cheeriest room in her late uncle's house, what he considered its heart.

A year and one day after Uncle Silas left this mortal coil, Marie made the decision to renovate and redecorate the front parlor. This shattered the one tenet he'd ever demanded she honor, but the sunniest room in the house had become the one least utilized and visited because of its austere presentation. And so, steeling herself, Marie took down photographs in frames, wrapping each in newspaper for removal to the attic. She ordered new furniture and decided eggshell paint would replace the beachy blue that had always been there.

With the front parlor emptied, she stared at the scuffed hardwood floor, still bearing its swirls of finger-paint like a poor man's version of *The Starry Night*. The first pang of guilt filled her gut. To Uncle Silas, those reminders of her presence had been just as worth preserving as the memory of Great Grandmother Van Horn or Wheezer the tortoiseshell cat, both of whom had lived and died before Marie was born.

She'd hire a man to sand the floor down, stain it in bright, blond urethane. Yes, but in so doing would erase part of herself and more of what made Silas such a good uncle. A *great* one, when she considered all he'd done for her throughout her life.

Again, she searched for signs of his ghost making good on his promise to return from the grave and wander the house to punish her for her crimes. None came, and that somehow made the results worse.

Her guilt doubled, turning solid and jagged in her stomach. Sleep became elusive. What had he asked of her, really? The front parlor—she'd viewed it as a mausoleum, but to him it had been a loving memorial to family. And that family deserved to be remembered.

Sick and bedraggled over what she'd started, Marie came to the conclusion that, indirectly, Uncle Silas had kept good on his promise—Marie *was* haunted, though not by his ghost. She cancelled the workmen and moved the old furniture back into the room and then returned the photographs to the walls, doing her best, through memory, to restore the room to its exact, former paradigm. The misery in her gut shorted out. For the first time in a week, she slept.

The next morning, sitting on the front parlor floor, she

opened the sketchpad, wet her fingers, and dipped them into the paint, making sure to get some on the scuffed antique hardwood.

4. Little Ghost
By Christina Chilelli

The empty house, so silent now. Nor was it ever a house filled with life, but it had your life. Your little energy, your constant presence. I left; you never did. When I returned, you were always there to greet me with joyous tirade, not permitting me for a moment to forget how much you missed me. Gone now, though, your wagging tail, your quiet excitement, and your unfailing desire to just be around me. Empty, barren, and feeling devoid of all purpose. For though the house remained, it seemed you took the home with you. That was something I could not reclaim. Just as I could not recover you.

We met on a telethon, those on TV. They always seemed so distant, but I met you that evening, so small and silent, accompanied by your two brothers. A wild mixture, an array none could ever truly guess. Some of this, some of that, a scrunched face, twisted leg, and green eyes. I wanted you; and the next day, I got you. I brought you home, made you my own, and raised you. There was an unfortunate encounter with some hot patio bricks when first you came to my home. A little dance, some pitiful whimpers, and I saved you.

I took you to the park. You in your prime, so happy and filled with life. We went with the younger brother, the sister, and the mother. St. Patrick's, perhaps, when the big fountain that shoots water up so high into the air, is dyed green. The tallest fountain in America, they say. You didn't care much about fountains. In fact, you hated water. You cared about the children. Others of your kind, you never got along with; but the children, they were all yours. They were smitten with you as well, which only served you all the better. They came to you wanting to pet and play, and you obliged them all.

It started a week before: a frantic call, leading to an impromptu trip to the vet. Your side, raw, bleeding, oozing. An inexplicable discovery that I was sure meant your decline. Hysteria in the office, thinking that your time was up. It was only a burst abscess though. Some antibiotics, pain meds, and you were sent home. You would heal, though they thought your skin would fall off of the area first. Frankenstein, I called you, since you were going to be shedding your skin. You were already my Gremlin but now took it one step further and became a true monster. You did not lose your skin though; and, instead, your wound healed well. So well that they were nothing but impressed. Everyone said how much better it looked.

It's quite now. Only the creak of the house to break the silence at night instead of your steady, rhythmic snoring laying beside my bed. The snurfle noise you made when breathing in. Gone. In its wake, only quiet.

I stand in the bathroom, in front of the big mirror putting my makeup on, trying to cover stubborn acne marks. In the past, the patter of your little feet would echo down the hall: the click of your claws on the tile, too long, needing to be trimmed again—a small transgression in its oversight, a massive sin against you when done.

I call out your name as though I expect you to respond. To somehow hear you stir, then come towards me, making your way around the corner to find me. I know you aren't there, not anymore; but just saying your name aloud, it breaks the silence. It helps me cope. Maybe I think that if you can hear me, see me, you will know how much I miss you.

But, in the absence of silence, comes the little *click, click, click*.

You were so stubborn. Almost impossible to housebreak. Perhaps it came from a certain laziness you always seemed to possess, even as a little thing. Impossible to know, much as it was impossible to know what you were, or where you came from. But you did not want to go outside.

You refused to use puppy pads and were locked in the bathroom most nights because you were not to be trusted outside of it. One night, as you developed a strange interest in the making of coffee, you were promised a taste of coffee grounds if only you let us sleep until after six. You delivered and were given coffee grounds in exchange. Who would believe it? You never bothered us while making coffee again.

It was my birthday, and I wanted to celebrate the both of us. You were my boy, after all, and I wanted everyone to acknowledge your birthday too. We threw a big party, and all the invitations had both our names on them, as well as both our ages. Some friends even brought you gifts too.

A big blow-up waterslide for me, which of course, when all were gone, became a curse for you. We never had a pool, and you had never been swimming, but I already knew you hated water. All the same, the blow-up pool was deep enough for me to put you in, and you would have to swim. I put you in, and held you as you padded through the water, attempting to doggy paddle. You swam a little, though not far; for I was fearful that your claws might puncture the inflated pool.

You never liked water. Nor did you like clothing. In water,

and in clothing, even a collar, you would simply freeze. It was your passive protest, a declining of movement that requested I free you from whatever I was currently subjecting you to. That was how I eventually learned to trim your nails and put you in the shower, for that forced you to stand still. But that day, you swam a little, just for me, for my birthday.

By Friday of that week, just five days later, you looked so much better. Your side was healing quickly, not nearly as bad as the vet thought; and you seemed as though you were much happier. They wouldn't need to see you back for a few months, and then it would just be a recheck of your cortisol meds to make sure everything was working properly. You were going to be fine.

Until you weren't... Monday afternoon, you started vomiting. I was a little concerned, just thinking that maybe you had an upset stomach from all the meds, but I took you to the vet right away. Why? Because your vomit was dark brown, and the vet was concerned that it might be blood. So I took you in, just in case, wanting to make sure you were okay, especially after the prior week's scare. I didn't really think, not truly, that it would be anything but a minor setback.

I walk through the empty house, tiled hallways fallen silent in your absence. I hear the click of your nails on occasion. Perhaps it is in my mind, just the glimmer of something that still remains. But I am unable to shake it. The sound feels so real, sounds so real.

I turn the corner to where you used to always lay in the office by the computer on a red cushion, and I swear I see you. I turn to get a full look at you, and then you vanish. But I could have sworn, if just for a second, that you were there; your little, tan body curled up with your tail around your legs. Your little scrunched face laying on your paws, looking up at me with your soulful little eyes watching me, wanting attention.

Yet when I turn to face you, you are already gone, as though you were never even there.

You were one popular little pup. It never mattered who it was, everyone wanted to pet the little thing and play with you. You were always so happy to be social, but also equally happy to play with people, bringing us toys, usually balls, sometimes even bigger than yourself. You taught yourself how to pick up the really big balls and would bring them to whoever was around, wanting us to throw, but not before they fought you for a slobber-covered ball hogged mostly by your mouth.

My aunts, they always liked you the best. You were so chill, mellow, always in search of attention. Content to just sit with them. Wherever you went, whoever you met, you were the favorite. The center of attention was always you. One time, we took you to the chiropractor with us, when you were just a puppy, in a build-a-bear rolling kennel; and some random guy took your picture because you were just so cute. That's how amazingly adorable you were. Some random guy wanted a picture of a random dog because you were just too lovable and sweet to resist.

We brought you to the vet again, though your usual vet was out of town. The vet tech came in, checked your gums, and she just made it seem as though something was wrong. A few minutes later, the vet herself made her appearance. She expressed a bit of concern, but not overly so, especially not after seeing your vomit, given that it wasn't blood. Still, she wanted to do a test to see if you were dehydrated, because your gums were a funny color, and your skin was not reacting properly to her pinching it.

A few minutes later, the vet came back with your test results. She explained to me how your body was low on red blood cells. Quite a bit low. She wanted to give you a few days to perhaps recover. But, if you had not started to recover in that time, we would have to either start a likely multi-thousand-dollar hunt for something that might not even be fixable… or put you down.

I collapsed. I couldn't imagine having to put you down, not

after you had been doing so much better. But that was our reality, and it's not as though they were going to tell their boss's stepdaughter to put down their dog unless they were really sure. I left that day knowing that tomorrow would likely be your last day, and that was a very hard burden to bear.

At night, in particular, when the house is quiet and there is no sound of your snoring, your little snurfly breath, your shifting. You are gone, but late at night, I don't feel like you are truly gone. In fact, I know you aren't.

When there is no one else around, I can feel you. When I am sad, it feels as though you are nearby, comforting me. It always gets cold when it seems as though you are around, watching over me, looking for scraps. Sometimes, it feels as though you are sniffing around my feet, the cold tile suddenly getting even colder.

The doorbell rings, and instead of your little howling bark, it is silent. But it is as though I can hear you still. More faintly, of course, as though you are bark howling from under a sheet in another room, but I can still hear you.

When sitting on the couch, it feels cold next to me. When you were alive, you would sit with your head on my leg, warming it. Now, it's the same spot, but this time… cold. Not overwhelmingly cold, just slightly. I can see I am alone, but it feels as though I'm not. As though you are still around, looking out for me. Always when I am the most alone, the saddest, that is when I know that you really are here. At first, I tried to pretend I was just imagining things. Since I know that was what it had to be. But slowly, I have begun to admit to myself that perhaps you are somehow still here.

When you were just a baby, you ended up so sick. So sick that we thought then we might have to put you down because we could not figure out what was wrong with you. They thought at first that it was parvo, but you tested negative. We took you to the vet, and they pumped you full of IV fluids and sent you home.

You had been pooping blood and vomiting nonstop for a day. Even in the midst of your illness you tried your best to go outside because you knew that was where you were supposed to go. But you were just too weak. However, you recovered.

But when we brought you home, you had a big hump on your back from all the fluids they gave you. It went away, rather quickly, but you did have it for a little while. Poor little baby. You almost died, but you fought through. You were always a fighter.

One thing that never changed about you, you loved to eat. No matter what I dropped on the floor, aside from a pretzel, you would eat it. I could never figure out why you didn't like pretzels. You just didn't.

Of course, all that eating got to you. You grew fat, really just so chunky. And I knew that I needed to get you to lose weight, otherwise you would not be healthy. So I started you with my sister's agility equipment. You actually loved to jump those little hurdles and got really good all around. I switched you to weight loss food and did everything I could to help you slim down.

You did, for a while. Then you got fat again. I mean sixteen pounds when you should have been twelve fat. But that was okay, because you were otherwise healthy. Until, without warning, you started to drink mass amounts of water and lost weight without exercising.

I took you to the vet, and they immediately told me things I already knew, that you were too thin now. It was crazy to see how fast you lost weight, and we could not figure it out. I tried to get you to gain weight, feeding you more and giving you peanut butter. Anything to get you to put on a few pounds.

They asked me to come in and work an extra shift that night, but I said I couldn't because it was my last night with you. I didn't know for sure, but at the same time... I did. I knew this was our last night together.

On the way home from school, I stopped and bought you

fries from McDonald's, your favorite food ever. You got so excited and stared at them as if they were your only true love. I gave you lots and even more affection.

Your breathing was so fast, just like your heartrate. You were so tired. I sat on the floor and did homework, even though my back was hurting, because I knew that this was my last chance to be with you. I laid next to you, snuggling you, your warm, bald skin between my fingers. You had lost so much hair. So much weight. But you were still my boy.

At first, it is just out of the corner of my eye. A brief glimpse of you on your red cushion as I walk by. The sight of you out of the corner of my eye, making me think you are there; but when I turn to really look at you, I am confronted with nothing but empty space.

Then, it changes. I come out of the bathroom, or the bedroom, and instead of being alone, you are right there. Standing, watching me, the slight wag of your translucent tail grabbing my attention. Only your nose and tail are really visible, with holes for your pale green eyes. It is you. I can feel it, but you have a white sheet draped over you as though it is Halloween. Maybe you have it to comfort me, make me feel at ease with your presence, just a little, nonthreatening ghost spending time with me.

You never really leave now. You follow me around, chasing after me with wagging tail and a spring in your step, your little sheet billowing behind you. I never have to feed you, though I have tried. Instead, you just stay around me, lay on my lap, and keep me company when I need it, when I feel the pain of your death the most keenly.

You hop up on the couch and place your light little head on my leg. You know that I need your love, your attention, and so, you are there for me. I can never really touch you, but I can feel your presence. Your fur is untouchable, unobtainable, but I know in my mind what it is supposed to be like. When I talk to you, you follow. You bound along behind me, beg for food, and sit next to me, just as you had before. It is as though it is the same, but I know it isn't, not really.

You were a fast-growing pup. It felt as though one day, you were a puppy, and the next, you were a dog, although you never really lost your puppiness. Not even when you were two, three, four, five, did you seem as though you were an adult and not a pup. Lively, filled with energy and excitement. You were the best little dog a person could ever ask for. I never wanted you to grow up, to grow old; and somehow, you managed to do all of the things I did not want. You grew up, you grew old; but I still loved you all the same.

There was nothing you would not have done for me, even as a pup. You were so loyal, so kind, and I could not imagine a better dog anywhere. You were the perfect puppy, and I very simply did not want you to be anything but a pup, though you became an even better adult.

Test after test after test after test, they finally diagnosed you. Cushing's disease. You had low Cortisol, and with medication, you would improve. Your energy would go up, your hair might even start to grow back. It meant constant monitoring, which was expensive; but at least you would feel much better and have a happier life.

So I agreed to do it for you. I knew it would be expensive between the medications and the tests, but it would be worth it if it made you feel better and helped you to live a healthier life. I wanted the best for you, and so I embarked on that quest. It helped, too. A few months in, you were playing with balls again, just like when you were a puppy. It made me so happy to see, brought me a fresh kind of joy realizing you were happy and feeling better.

I sat in the office, you on my lap, my mom next to me, keeping it together as best I could. I didn't want your life to end with you remembering me crying and sobbing. I wanted you to be happy, comfortable. I wanted you to feel loved, to know how much I cared about you, not be concerned for me, or afraid. We got the news from the vet, and it was what we thought. You were done; there was nothing more we could do for you. It was the best thing we could do to let you go, but that was a nearly impossible feat. I didn't want you to go. I wanted you to stay my little pup forever.

They gave us time alone. My mom even left to give me a private moment with you. I hugged you tight and sobbed briefly before I pulled myself together and calmed down. I had to be calm, for you. I told you how much I cared about you, loved you, and let them all come back. I wouldn't give you to my mom for more than a minute since she was sobbing, and I didn't want you to be scared or upset. The vet came back in, and I put you on my lap.

I bent over you, hugging you close, and nodded to the vet. They gave you some saline, then some propofol. It took you a minute, but your eyes started to flutter. I whispered what a good boy you were again and again, telling you how much I loved you. She gave you the final injection. It wasn't obvious at first, and I kept telling you how much I loved you. She checked your heart again and again and finally told us you were gone.

It may stem from stress, or anxiety, or simple grief. It is never really you that I see. Echoes of a happier time, a time past perhaps, a time gone. You are never there, and I know you are not, but I wish to cling to your memory all the same. If time were altered and the present kinder, you would still be with me. But you are not, and so I must learn to live without you, though your memory will never grow dim in my mind.

5. Jeffery Norman, the Brother Who Planted True Reminders
By David Singer

At 43 years of age, my brother died. Technically gone, he periodically returns to express his love. Early on, he seeded a trail of messages to find through others. Later he simply showed up. I think he has one more trick up his sleeve. My name is David Singer. I am 76 and still feel as if my younger brother Jeff will return shortly from his vacation. All the events herein are real. The messages contained are my brother's, not mine.

At first, I just wanted to be angry and wanted the record to be set straight. The Orange County Coroner knew this and stared me in the eye. His initial letter was cold and unflattering.

"Your brother was an alcoholic and a drug addict. He died because he had no liver left worthy of an autopsy."

I tossed back, "The operative word here is *was*. Did you do a blood tox screen?"

"I didn't need to. He was a drunk and a druggie."

"Do a tox test, as required by law, and you will only isolate nicotine and traces of the pain med he ran out of. He was found between two cars in the parking lot of a pharmacy, yes?"

"That is in the police report. I believe he was shooting up."

"Let us consider your opinion, shall we? You are saying that, maybe after he died, he put the needle and syringe in a sharp's container? Healed the jab wound? Cleaned up the blood spatter? None of those considerations are in the police report."

"I might have overlooked that omission. We are pretty busy if you haven't noticed."

"Ah, right, too busy for facts. Okay, let me fill in some details for you. Jeffrey Norman died just before he could get his meds, died in a pharmacy parking lot seeking help. He had in his pockets a set of building keys, his prescription, his weekly paycheck, and exact cash for the bill. Not one piece of druggie thingies. Earlier, at 3:30pm when he closed up his employer's book binding shop, locked the place, and got on his bicycle, Jeffrey was a twenty-mile peddle away from the pharmacy. His bicycle is in the police report. The second thing of note is that any other bike would have been stolen, but not this one. It was *Jeff's Bike*, and everybody knows *you don't mess with Jeff's stuff*. Sir, Jeffrey Norman was peddling the day he died, not shooting up."

The coroner dropped his eyes to some paperwork on his desk.

"Your brother is dead from extreme liver damage, proximal cause being decades of drug and alcohol abuse." He looked back up, stared into my eyes, softened his demeanor, then asked, "Why should I put his body through expensive tests we apply to murders? Do you have any idea how many dead people we process a month in Orange County? Thousands! Quite frankly, the fact your brother could peddle a bicycle a block, much less twenty miles, astounds me. He committed suicide by crapping out his liver. Drugs and alcohol. The man killed himself. That is my official finding and what will go into my official report."

I looked at the clock. Four more minutes remained of the promised five he agreed to, so I persisted.

"For the record then." I leaned across his desk and switched on his Official Orange County Coroner Voice Recorder, "My name is David Michael, the older brother of deceased Jeffrey Norman, and I am here to state the rest of his story."

Two weeks ago, my brother died in an early-aborted attempt to live a normal life. I tracked the paycheck to the employing temp agency and showed up to ask where he was working. They requested identification and my purpose of visit. The entire office burst into tears when I mentioned Jeffrey Norman's death. One by one, each reminded me of his power of encouragement and hope for the future. They explained Jeffrey Norman worked for an ultra-high-end book bindery shop. The keys were to the building, an astonishing fact for a mere temporary employee. Jeff had never told me this, never bragged of position; but he did say he was finally happy.

Humbled, I located his employer and introduced myself.

The employer called in his small crew and proceeded to excuse them for the rest of the day as a tribute to my brother.

Alone with me, the employer confided, "Jeff was undoubtedly the best leather-binding man since Gutenberg invented the press. His works are art on display in The Huntington Library and The Smithsonian. I gave only him the priceless books because he was the one man alive who could raise them from the dead. Truly, if you want to remember your brother, visit either museum. His works will call to you like pearls washed up on the shore of *The Sea of Mediocracy.*"

I handed over the keys, which I presumed were his because I knew Jeffrey Norman was homeless.

The owner stared at the keys in his palm. "So much like Jeff. Even as a dead man, he has managed to return what is not his." He clinked the keys on the desktop, then continued, "This shop survives by using hand tools from antiquity, each being museum pieces in their own right. The first day he walked in was the last day we suffered any theft. Jeff handled each and every tool as if they were his children and taught the rest of my people why the tools deserved great respect and love. I handed him the keys to my life and was planning on handing him the business when I retired."

When I quietly departed, the owner was silently staring at the set of keys, glistening with the splash of his tears.

I knew my brother lived in a camp somewhere in what was then the extensive undeveloped wilderness of Orange County. No street address was available, so I approached as many homeless people as I could, asking if they knew where.

"East of here, I'm pretty sure."

I went east and asked.

"Just a bit north of here. Big California oak tree. Can't miss it."

I went north and asked at an encampment.

"Over there. Under that oak. But don't go there. Nobody messes with Jeff's stuff."

"I'm his brother. Did you know him?"

"Um, yes. What do you mean, *did you know him*? Has something happened to Jeff?"

"Jeffrey Norman died a few days ago."

The entire encampment went silent. A man and a woman, apparently the spokespeople, approached to join me and the first man.

"Bummer, man. What the fuck are we going to do without him?"

The woman spoke through tears. "We lose our jobs, lose our homes, and now we lose our inspiration."

She turned and walked away, muttering, "Crap! Crap! Crap! Crap! Crap!"

The two men walked me to Jeff's camp. The place was outdoors but arranged like a studio suite. Memories flooded back from sharing childhood bedrooms. His clothes hung in an orderly fashion under a tarp, exactly as he always insisted in his closets. His suit coat on the left, his dress pants to the immediate right, followed by several dress shirts, then informal clothing likewise assembled as if he had been there mere moments ago to straighten everything in preparation for my visit. Underneath were his mirror-polished shoes reflecting sunlight, then loafers, then the spot reserved for his work tennies that he had on his feet when he died. Above them was the empty slot for his work clothes last worn in the parking lot to his pharmacy of choice.

I knew what to expect, turned to where his deck would be, saw a battered table on top of which was a pen-pencil mug, a small battery lamp for night work, a box of writing paper, and a row of his favorite books kept upright by two polished brass ass-ended elephants triumphantly trumpeting defiance to the sky.

A folding wooden camp chair for sitting. A hammock for sleeping. And, of course, a small couch for the comfort of guests. I turned more. A small kitchenette with a Primus stove, then one pot, one plate, one cup, one each of knife, fork, and spoon, all arranged in a small dish drainer, nicely dried from his final washup after his final breakfast. Instant coffee. A cooler once full of ice, now just warm water suitable for washing. I hated to dump it out, hearing my brother admonish me for wasting precious water in a desert. He would find a way to shower with it or clean his clothes. I wished he were there to show me how.

"Well, he's not coming back, so take what you want," I said.

The men looked at each other and shook their heads. One said, "Dude, you don't understand. We got respect. *Nobody messes with Jeff's stuff.*"

I found Jeff's stash of cash. Not much. Technically, he owed me $200 from years back. I thumbed through the bills. Enough to cover the debt and a bit left over. I kept the $200 to be split between Jeff's two daughters, then handed what remained to the men.

"Jeff is grateful for your neighborliness and good will."

They refused the money.

I added the $200.

They refused the money.

"Look," I said, "the money cannot be split evenly. One hundred to each of his girls, sure; but then there is this pocket-burning cash that screws everything up. Do Jeff a favor and take it off my hands."

I set the remainder on the table.

"Be a shame if the wind blows it away."

I gathered his clothes and shoes, Nobody there would wear any of it, respect being a hard affliction to overcome; so I hauled them to the Salvation Army where I knew Jeff had a weekend night gig.

As far as I know, Jeff's camp is still out there waiting for the next generation of homeless or the next massive housing development, whichever comes first.

My final stop was the Salvation Army facility. I donated the clothes.

"Hey! What the fuck??? These belong to Jeffrey Norman!"

"I know. I'm his brother. He won't be needing them any longer and wants somebody here to benefit."

The woman returned with a large box. She gently set the clothes and shoes inside.

"I'll send them to the store. They'll sell quickly there." She looked me in the eye and said, "Around here, nobody messes with Jeff's stuff."

I was leaving when a raggedy guy sidled up to me.

"You his brother? Is he really, um, you know?"

My heart was growing heavier with every person I told, a truth they did not want to hear. *Damnit Bro, why did you go and do this to me?*

"Yeah."

"Well, I just wanted to say he was something special. You do know they lock us in this joint after they feed us, right? We gotta do religious stuff in exchange for the food and a place to sleep. Lot of the people here don't want to keep their end of the bargain, so the locks get thrown and the doors get guarded. Now, Jeff, he is one of the gate keepers." He pointed to a side door. "That's his exit. The place catches on fire, he springs us loose. Otherwise, we supposed to be sleeping like babies until breakfast. No smoking allowed inside. But Jeff? He got a key to that door, and us who gonna die if we don't get at least one puff a night, Jeff steps outside with us, just one at a time, chats while we smoke, then unlocks the door and ushers us back in."

He looked around as if maybe the FBI was listening in.

"I gotta tell you, Jeff is the best counselor ever! Makes it worthwhile to be locked up for a night."

My brother, The Age of Aquarius in his one-man off-Broadway show.

Whodathunk?

I was still in the coroner's office, setting the official record straight about Jeffrey Norman. I noted by the clock that I had 15 seconds time remaining, so I made my final statement.

"My brother was a tax-paying citizen who probably was more influential than any of your petty politicians to whom you pander for budget pennies. Jeffrey Norman deserves what the law requires. Give the man a proper autopsy so he does not go on record as just another homeless, wasted, alcoholic, druggie. He left a lasting legacy of good, despite early-life decisions that proved fatal in his forties."

I switched off the recorder, stood, and left the office, the building, and Orange County.

About a year later, the family gathered off the Oregon coast to spread the ashes of Jeff the son, brother, husband, father. Jeff reasoned that over time, parts of him would eventually seep to every salt-water body on the planet. *Jeffrey Norman on his World Tour, coming to a beach near you sometime soon.*

When I returned home, I faced surgery for a potentially fatal disease. The office phone rang on one of the incoming lines, but nobody picked up. So, uncustomarily, I answered. The voice on the line said, "I heard you are going under the knife. I ask only one thing of you. Don't die."

The call dropped. I was staring into the handset when a co-owner happened to walk by.

"Who was that?" she asked.

I set the phone down and replied, "Jeffrey Norman. He requested that I not die in surgery."

She blinked.

"But, he's dead."

I closed my eyes.

"Kinda hard to explain, isn't it?"

A few months later, having survived the surgery and busy working through recovery, I pulled a load of laundry out of the washer. Usually, one of my socks gets eaten if I don't count, so I was not surprised to get an odd number. What was odd was that it was one more sock, not one less. I sorted the socks.

Nearly two years after giving away his clothes on the other side of the country, one of Jeff's camp socks emerged from my washing machine.

I have since held on to that silly sock, knowing that the day after I toss it, my brother will make sure the other shows up. Both scenarios improbable, but there we are.

Several years later I had a "change of personal administrations" and followed the new leadership to North Carolina where I also had a total change of occupation. I became a sailmaker. As such, I was invited onto a team that attempted to sail from Beaufort, NC to St. Martin on a thirty-seven-foot Tartan. Blue water sailing, they call it. Out with the big boys on the vast ocean where there is no cell service, no hospitals, no rescue service, no cops, just pirates and beautifully unforgiving Mother Nature.

I had the midnight-to-three watch. I was at the helm coming out of one gale and sure to hit the next, steering by the stars because we were deep in the Bermuda Triangle with a malfunctioning autopilot, a busted food freezer, a burnt-out alternator, and a dead radio. Bermuda was closer than turning back. We barely missed getting sliced in half by the only other private sailboat on the entire Atlantic Ocean, a Hinkley 40 abandoned by the occupants during the previous storm: one with crushed ribs, another drowned, one survivor, all three professional licensed sea captains.

It was a little after one in the morning when my brother, Jeffrey Norman, materialized on the leeward side of the cockpit, sitting with his legs out, arms stretched over the seatback, head facing into the wind and spray, perilously close to the cold ocean waters racing by, and, of course, without a personal flotation device on his body.

My initial comment was, "It will be a lot safer and more comfortable to sit on the starboard side, up here to windward."

He said, "And good to see you to, bro. It's been a while since I sailed with you. Where was that? South San Fran bay? Climb up there to sit? Naw, I think I will stay down here. I want the chance to feel spray on my face and the blood-rush of recklessly plowing through turgid water at night like a blind bull."

He mentioned the autopsy. One had finally been done. "I do not fault the coroner. He was desperately cutting corners like a ten-year-old foolishly trying to stretch an easy single into the game-winning inside-the-park home run. I watched for two weeks inside that ice box drawer. I'm thinking he had a budget problem, so thanks for getting it sorted out."

I suppose that settled things in his mind because we pressed through the angry Atlantic in further silence save for the wail of the wind, the hiss of the water sweeping by, and the drum of the hull pounding into the oncoming waves. There we were, brothers again.

In time, he stood. "I guess this is it. Take care, bro."

He pivoted like a ball player. Then he stepped off the boat and dematerialized.

Every drop of salt water that touches my face returns the memory of that final brotherly sail. As I wait for the other sock to drop, I shall be forever racing for the endless love given by a brother I never deserved.

6. The Recluse
by Sara Fowles

The lights were flickering again in the silent, dusty house; and Eldon Greenfield wondered for the umpteenth time if the disturbance was a ghost or an electrical problem. He squinted up at the bronze chandelier above the kitchen island. Pots and pans hung on hooks which ringed the light fixture. They always reminded him of Nellie. If he closed his eyes, he could conjure the phantom savory smells that had once wafted from those pieces of cookware. More than forty years' worth of home-cooked meals shared in the old farmhouse, he reckoned.

One by one, each lightbulb winked at him. He rubbed his eyes with calloused knuckles. A popping sound accompanied sudden darkness from one of the four bulbs. The others blazed steadfast once again.

Eldon hoped it wasn't electrical. He couldn't fix it himself, but he certainly couldn't call a repair person. No one had set foot in the house, besides a couple of interloping raccoons, in five years.

Nellie would have gotten a kick out of the raccoons. *Probably would have tried to feed 'em*, he thought. He chuckled, imagining her bringing tiny plates of her special pot roast to the attic. When those critters appeared, he didn't bother calling Animal Control. It would have been a hassle to speak to strangers and answer all their pestering questions. Easier to leave the creatures be.

Leave the world alone and hope it would do the same for him. That had been his philosophy since his wife died. He wanted nothing to do with people anymore. Nellie had been the one to invite guests into their home, socialize with the neighbors, and go out into town to immerse herself in the small-town culture. Not him. He kept to himself, and he liked it that way.

Nellie sure did know how to throw a party though. No doubt about that. Every guest would leave flushed and full from the libations and the feast. Eldon did his best to come out of his shell and mingle, but he always found himself with his hands in his pockets, staring at the floor in a corner. Truth be told, his favorite part was the end of the evening, the quiet after all the noise, when he and Nellie would sit close together in the kitchen and drowsily pick at the last of the pie. There was always pie.

Eldon cast a vacant stare toward the pots and pans. He thought they swayed, ever so slightly. But maybe he imagined it. When he looked more closely, he saw the outline of a cobweb. He didn't cook much anymore—in fact, he couldn't remember the last proper meal he had eaten. Nellie's food had been the glue that held their lives together. Now he was bone thin.

The lights flickered, an all too familiar occurrence as of late. It had begun a week ago, mostly in the kitchen and the bedroom. In the bedroom, it was more pronounced. While Eldon lay sleeping, in the dead of night, the lamp beside his bed would snap on, startling him awake. He had never been a sound sleeper. After a few times, he unplugged the lamp. It still turned on. That was when he first thought it could be a ghost.

Much like the raccoons, if it were a ghost, he would leave it be. Part of him hoped it was a spirit of some kind—a presence to fill the empty space in the house. It might keep him company a bit.

All the benefits of a live person without the annoyance of small talk and social etiquette.

He turned his thoughts over and leaned heavily against the counter.

"I sure do miss you, Nellie," Eldon spoke, and his lips cracked when they parted. His voice rasped from disuse.

Another bulb flared, popped, and went dark. The two that remained grew brighter.

He tilted his head and stared, agog. "Well, damn."

Maybe a ghost would be just the thing.

The next morning, Eldon shuffled straight to the kitchen with a horrible headache and a melancholy he couldn't shake.

As soon as he sat down on the counter stool, the two lightbulbs above the island burst to life with the faint hiss of electric charge. He looked up, but the brightness hurt his eyes. Slouching, he pressed his fingers to his temples.

"Not now," he said.

The lights, obstinate, pulsed with a yellow-white glow. When he closed his eyes, he could still see the halos from the bulbs.

"Please," he groaned, eyelids squeezed shut.

Pop.

Another bulb out. One left. He dared a quick peek. The sole survivor was the light closest to the hook bearing the stockpot. Many a soup had been made in that vessel. Italian wedding was always Nellie's favorite, though Eldon preferred plain tomato.

A soup doesn't need frills, he used to say.

Nellie would quote Virginia Woolf and claim that she couldn't get a good night's sleep or clear her head without "dining well," which to her meant Italian wedding soup.

Eldon's retort contained his own wisdom: *Yes, but if we don't use those tomatoes, they'll go bad.*

When she cooked, she wore an old-fashioned yellow linen

apron tied around the neck and the waist. Now it hung in the walk-in pantry; and when he went in there, he touched the material and told her hello. Grief was like that.

The last remaining light—the sole survivor, just like him— winked at him. Acting on instinct, he winked back.

The light flickered and didn't stop. He blinked both eyes rapidly until he felt like a fool.

"This sure is a fine chat," he said to the bulb. "Should've learned Morse code. Then we could communicate properly."

The light snapped off. The darkness settled around him.

He stood and began to pace.

Eldon endured a long coughing fit as he wiped away more dust from the bookshelves. Nellie used to keep up with the cleaning. She had a special rag for dusting and some lemon-scented spray. Eldon just used his sleeve. What did it matter? It wasn't as if he dressed to impress anyone. He believed clothes were for function, not fashion.

He smiled, remembering the way Nellie would lay out a combination of shirt and slacks for him whenever they planned to venture into town. She even placed a pair of shoes beside the bed to complete the ensemble. Even though he groused about it, he understood why she did it. The town gossip had been abuzz one January with the story of how Eldon Greenfield bought groceries wearing his pajamas, fishing boots, and a shower cap.

Nellie had been mortified. She was sick in bed that day, and Eldon explained that was the reason he donned the crazy getup. His mind was fractured with worry, and he had little awareness of what he put on as he dashed out the door into a heavy downpour. He just meant to keep dry.

"Don't fret so much about me," Nellie had said, and later it became a refrain. As she lost her strength, gradually, Eldon paid even less attention to his clothing. By that time, Nellie didn't notice either.

Then there had come the day he had to get dressed up one last time. After that, Eldon retreated into the life of a solitary man. When he went into town wearing bathrobes or mismatched, tattered outfits, no one said a word.

Eldon sneezed, and the dust brought him out of his reverie. He turned his focus back to the old bookcase in front of him. Reminiscing about Nellie's soup had prompted him to search for her cookbooks, but so far he hadn't found them. Nothing but the novels from her literature classes and a few insect husks tucked away between the paperbacks.

As he crouched to examine the bottom shelf, he felt something solid and heavy connect with the back of his head. For a moment, he saw stars.

Stunned, he located the object that struck him lying face up beside him on the floor. It was a book, though not the one he'd been looking for.

"Well, I'll be damned," he said as he examined the title.

Making Morse Code Easy: Start Today!

Yes. He surely would.

"Let's try again, old friend," Eldon spoke to the lightbulb, which pulsated in its usual manner. "I think I've learned enough. Why don't we start with some pleasantries. How do you do?"

He had carefully rehearsed what to say after he mastered the basics of Morse code. It didn't take long. He was a quick study; and his grandfather, who had been in the Navy, gave him some lessons when he was young, which came back to him once he sorted out the *dits* and *dahs*. Though he pondered many options of how to approach communicating with the lightbulb ghost, he settled on the things he imagined Nellie would tell him to say.

Introduce yourself and offer a polite greeting. He could hear her now, but he'd forgotten the introduction. *Try again.*

"Hello up there. I am Eldon Paul Greenfield. Son of Chester. And Marianne, but she died giving birth to me, so I never met her." He faltered. The ghost didn't need to know all that. "Pardon me. I just meant to say pleasure to make your acquaintance."

He waited. The light stopped its persistent flicker and went still. For a long moment, he perched on the edge of his seat, teeth clenched. Then something happened.

Blink-blink-blink-blink. Pause. *Blink-blink.*

Eldon sat back in his chair, incredulous. The light burned strong.

He scrambled for his chart. Four short blinks, then two more. *Dit-dit-dit-dit. Dit-dit.* His mind raced to translate.

H-I. Hi.

"Hi!" he shouted. "You said hi!" He clapped his hands and whooped.

The light shone. He stared.

What if it was a coincidence? The damn bulb had done nothing but act faulty. The timing of the off-and-on beats could have been a fluke. Just an electrical issue.

Only one thing to do. He drew in a breath.

"Excuse me. I don't mean to trouble you, but . . . did you say hello to me?"

Immediately, it started up again. He paid attention to the length of each blink.

Dah . . . dit-dah . . . dah. Dit. Dit-dit-dit.

His fingers flew along the Morse code chart of dots and dashes, the symbols that could make it possible for the living and the dead to converse. The ghost in the light had spelled a single word.

Yes.

Raccoons roamed throughout the house, and it was raining inside. Eldon exited the bedroom, blinked, and found himself in the bright kitchen. All the bulbs were lit up in an angelic glow, and beneath them stood his Nellie.

He took in the sight of her in her yellow apron, waist trim and cheeks flushed. She appeared just as she did when they first got married, beaming, full of exuberance.

"Get your buns over here, mister, and give me a smooch!" she said.

Dutifully, he complied with an eager grin. Her lips were soft and warm.

When he pulled back, his mouth felt wet. He touched his fingertips to his lips. They came away covered in a sticky, red substance.

Blood? Eldon panicked.

Nellie placed a hand on his arm. "Tomato soup," she said and gestured to the pot on the stove.

He could smell it. With a flourish, he produced a long-handled utensil from behind his back.

"You'll need this sooner or ladle," he teased. One of his signature bad puns.

She took it from him, laughed, and stirred the soup. A perfect moment.

Eldon moved to sit down at the counter only to discover a piping hot pie had been placed on the stool. He took a step back to admire the latticework of the homemade crust.

But what was that? The pie bulged, and a red liquid oozed out, trickling onto the seat.

Warily, he regarded Nellie.

"Just the cherry filling," she said, but her eyes watered, and her voice sounded an octave too high.

He looked on in horror as she coughed up blood. That sound played in his head night and day, even infiltrating his dreams.

"I'm sorry, Nellie," he said.

"Who are you? I don't know you." Her expression was blank, her tone hollow.

Suddenly, she was dumping all of the soup into a suitcase.

"What are you doing?"

"I have to go now," she answered simply.

"But I don't want you to leave."

She was already gone.

Eldon woke up with the feeling of all his bones turned to lead, including his skull. He struggled to lift his head from the sweat-drenched pillow.

When he finally sat up, his eyes snapped to the objects at the foot of the bed.

Folded neatly on top of the comforter were a pair of brown corduroy pants and a beige cable knit sweater.

"Morning, Peg," Eldon said to the lightbulb a week later. He wasn't sure if it was short for Peggy. Peg was all the spirit had spelled when he asked its name.

The light remained off.

"Don't feel like talking today?" he prompted. After the week of nightmares he'd endured, he surely could use a friend; and since he hadn't spoken to a living soul in years, Peg was all he had.

In the few short conversations they'd had through Morse code, he found an ease and rhythm that always eluded him with real, live human beings, who tended to make him nervous.

Nellie used to worry about him. She'd tell him to try to make friends, that connections with other people would keep him afloat when the hard times tried to drown him.

Now here he was without any companions, and the life raft that presented itself was a ghost.

Peg.

Part of him had hoped it was Nellie. When he found his going-into-town clothes on the bed, he wished for it fervently; but when he asked for a name, the light denied him hers.

Still, Peg was someone to talk to, he mused. He shared stories about his life, and Peg listened, providing the occasional comment—usually only one or two words, but it was enough.

You rascal, she spelled on one occasion when he told her about stealing his dad's Impala before he even had his license, just to impress Linda Wingate.

Good man, Peg spelled after he confided that he sat with Old Blue all night after the fireworks when the basset hound was scared and restless.

Eldon realized he actually looked forward to his kitchen chats with the unseen visitor. It didn't matter that he couldn't look into Peg's eyes. Her words were enough.

But today, she wasn't speaking. The light showed no signs of life.

"Hello there, Peg," he tried again.

Darkness prevailed.

Eldon moved toward the wall and did something he hadn't done in weeks. He turned on the light switch.

The light snapped on as expected, and he returned to his seat beneath the bulb.

"There now," he said. "You have anything to say?" A hint of desperation crept into his voice. "I hoped we could have a chat. I'm still having those dreams about Nellie, and . . ." He trailed off, realizing he was only talking to himself.

A few more minutes passed. The light burned steady. No disturbance, electrical or otherwise.

Eventually, Eldon dragged his feet back over to the wall and turned the light off with a soft click.

Dusk had settled, enveloping the quiet corners of the house, as Eldon roused himself from the bedroom floor. He had crawled there and pulled his cable knit sweater over his shoulders and torso like a blanket.

Rubbing his eyes, he sat up and stretched his old joints until they popped, one at a time, loosening.

"Sleeping on the floor's a young man's game," he grumbled to himself.

Automatically, he stumbled to the kitchen before remembering: Peg had stopped talking.

He slumped at the counter, forlorn.

Blink . . . blink. Blink! Blink!

There she was! Eldon gasped, then lunged for his chart and pen.

The blinking continued, and his fingers ached as he struggled to keep up. A furiously scrawled line of dots and dashes took shape as Eldon transcribed the bulb's signals.

Soon, he realized that there was a repeating pattern on the page. The same two words spelled out over and over. The back of his neck went cold.

He knocked over his stool as he recoiled. Stifling a frightened cry, he stared at the message.

GET OUT.

Eldon didn't mind sitting in the dark. He thought back to the evening after the funeral when he'd come home and turned on every single light in each and every room. Somehow, he hoped it would comfort him, but with the emptiness laid bare to his raw eyes, he only felt more alone.

The dark was more like a blanket that concealed the truth. He could hide there and pretend things were different.

This time, he put on the clothes, even though the corduroy pants fit loosely now. The sweater felt the same. He lay on his side on top of the comforter, the bed creaking in the same way it had for years.

"Get out," he whispered. "But where would I go?"

The sound of knocking stirred him from his slumber. It echoed all around him, so he wasn't sure if it came from the walls or the ceiling, but it did seem contained to the bedroom.

He swung his legs over the side of the bed and placed his feet on the floor. His left toe poked at something. Squinting, he discerned a shoe. A pair of his fine brown shoes, the ones that went with the sweater and pants he was wearing now. He put them on without thinking twice.

"Nellie," he said out loud, but the pounding in the walls drowned him out.

"Stop, please," he said.

Knock-knock. Knock! Knock!

"Peg, or whoever—whatever you are, I don't want any trouble." As he spoke to the walls, he moved out into the hallway, inching toward the front of the house.

Knock. Knock! Knock!

He paused at the end of the hallway. *Wait a minute. It's still doing Morse code!*

Eldon ducked out of the hall and into the spare room, covering his ears.

"Go away!" he yelled. "Be quiet!"

Faintly, he could still hear it. He listened closely. The last sequence of knocks was three dashes, he was almost positive. The letter "O." Was it spelling "get out" again?

The same pattern repeated. Another "O."

Unable to help himself, he tried to decipher the letters, but without his chart, he was lost. All he could make out were more "O's" and a couple of "L's."

Overwhelmed, Eldon slunk farther into the spare room. He thought he heard the sound going on, but it was his heartbeat pulsing in his ears.

A small stack of items drew his attention to the corner of the room. There were so many old memories tucked away in there. Photo albums, books, and containers. After a moment's consideration, he approached and reached for the box on top. It had been months since he'd looked inside.

He called it his "sad box," and it originally held the pair of brown shoes he now wore. In it was a collection of sympathy cards, letters, newspaper clippings, and some prayer cards. "Forever in our hearts" was inscribed on the laminated keepsake.

When he dug deeper, there were older anniversary and birthday cards from Nellie, love letters they'd exchanged when they started dating, and other special things.

Eldon dropped to his knees and methodically went through every saved piece of paper. Halfway to the bottom, he discovered the poem Nellie had written him for their wedding day. With tear-stung, bleary eyes, he read it.

> *Dear Eldon—*
> *My beam of bright, exquisite light,*
> *More true than stars above,*
> *My anchor through the darkest night,*
> *To you I pledge my love.*
>
> *—Yours, now and forever,*
> *Penelope Elizabeth Miller (soon to be Greenfield!)*

She had drawn a heart next to her name—her real name, which he hadn't used in all the time he'd known her because she had always been his Nellie.

The forceful pounding resounded throughout the house. The noise came from all around him. He held his head in his hands and rocked back and forth. As if in response, the knocking grew softer, gentler.

Tracing his fingers over her written words, his thumb caressed the phrase "exquisite light."

Then he looked again at her signature. *Soon to be Greenfield.* "Penelope. Elizabeth. Greenfield," he whispered, and he knew, and the walls rejoiced, sounding like thunder, like drums, like love.

"I'm listening now!" he called out. "I'm sorry!"

The knocking ceased.

He was on his feet. "Talk to me, my love!"

The silence stretched.

"Nellie! I didn't know it was you!"

Only his heartbeat filled the void. Eldon looked all around the room, as if she might appear.

The light, he thought, and he ran toward it. When he reached the kitchen, he wasted no time in snapping on the switch.

Pop.

"No!" he cried.

The last bulb had gone out.

A few minutes later, Eldon finally found what he was looking for after rummaging through a junk drawer near the sink. It was the last one left in the house.

He cradled the 40-watt bulb like an egg taken from a bird's nest, protectively. With great care, he removed the old lightbulb and screwed in the new one.

There wasn't a moment's pause before the blinking started up, and he scrambled for his pen and chart.

"Okay, okay, love," he said under his breath as he made hasty marks to denote the *dits* and *dahs* that would deliver his wife's words to him.

E-L, he recognized right away, followed by D-O-N. His name.

He concentrated so that he wouldn't miss anything. After

more than a dozen letters had been recorded, he double-checked the pauses and separation of the words.

"Well, I'll be," he said with a rising smile.

He had his message; his instructions, as they were.

Old fool. Get out. See people.

A loud snap echoed, as the new bulb, too, went dark. His eyes widened.

"But I just got you back!" Eldon protested. "Can you knock again instead? Nellie, please?"

Nothing.

He folded his arms around himself, unsure what to do. The material of his sweater was soft.

"More lightbulbs," he muttered. "Just need to run to the store."

After all, he decided, he was already dressed, even down to the shoes.

Resolved, Eldon Greenfield prepared himself to take the road he hadn't traveled in years and go into town.

The wind slapped his cheeks like an admonishment as soon as he stepped outside. Eldon realized he hadn't taken a coat, and it was near November. A swath of leaves blanketed his yard in reds and oranges, stretching out to the road and beyond.

He ducked back inside and grabbed an old flannel hanging in the front closet.

"Be right back, Nellie," he said softly before the door creaked closed.

This time when he emerged and started down the long dirt driveway, a group of kids passed by on the street a hundred feet away. Eldon squinted as he moved closer but didn't recognize any of them. He wondered if any of their parents used to come to Nellie's parties.

A blonde pixie of a girl ran, laughing, between two red-haired boys. They all appeared to be about ten or eleven years old. Ten years ago, Eliza Hargrove had a baby, he suddenly remembered. The girl could be hers. And the boys could be part of the McAllister brood, he supposed.

Eldon meandered down the driveway, lost in thought about all the people he used to know. Who else might he see in town? Maybe Bill at the hardware store if he still worked there. Or Mrs. Grover. He gulped. She was a hugger, and she wore too much perfume. If he didn't evade her, he would end up smelling like a flower dipped in formaldehyde.

At some point during his approach, Eldon realized the kids were whispering and pointing back toward his house. He was a few paces behind them, and they didn't seem to have noticed him.

". . . and everyone says it's haunted," the tiny blonde was saying.

"It is!" one of the boys cut in. "You can see the lights turning off and on at night."

"Shut up, liar!" the other boy said and gave him a shove.

"It's true!" he insisted.

Eldon leaned forward, straining to hear. The kids continued to walk, adopting a brisker pace.

"Remember there was that big fire there when we were in first grade?" the little girl said, before her voice was carried off by the wind.

Eldon caught only the end of the conversation. ". . . before we see a ghost!"

The three children took off running and shrieking, in terror or delight—he couldn't tell which.

A strange sensation prickled at the back of his neck, and he had the feeling there was something he was forgetting.

He glanced back at his house—at the siding, once white, now weathered and streaked with black. The house looked back at him, solemn, empty, and dark.

That was it. Lightbulbs. Now if only he could remember what happened to his car.

Eldon trudged down the road, farther from home than he'd been in years. He'd located the car in the garage, but the tires had deflated, and he couldn't recall where he'd left his keys anyway.

He thought about what those kids had said about a fire. The tickle at the back of his neck crawled up over his scalp. Now he was certain he should remember something. Concentrating, he thought back to the years after Nellie had died, how he'd wandered through the house, lost, unsure what to do. He belonged with Nellie, but she was somewhere he couldn't go. Unable to follow, he found himself tethered to the house where so many memories lingered.

He remembered roaming the house, wailing, unending blank hours. No matter how hard he tried, he couldn't conjure any details about a fire. The children must have been mistaken.

Threading his way through the streets that led to town, he remained tucked into the shadows of evening. He listened to the human sounds, the signs of life, drifting out of open garages and windows. Families bickered, laughed, ran water, or clanked pots and pans. *Doing the after-supper dishes*, he reasoned. Pumpkins and bowls of candy adorned doorsteps, and that was when he figured out that today must be Halloween.

Soon the neighborhood would be filled with trick-or-treaters. The hardware store might even close early for the holiday. As Eldon walked, he continued to think about the town and the people in it, all living their ordinary lives.

He passed another house with eggshell-blue shutters. A peal of giggling emerged from an open front door, and a couple of teenagers spilled out, engrossed in conversation. Closing his eyes, he took in the rise and fall of their voices. It sounded musical, and he smiled. For the first time, he wanted to strike up a conversation with a stranger. The urge overpowered him. Oddly, out here, surrounded by them, the idea of meeting new people didn't terrify him; in fact, it even seemed . . . nice.

I can wave at these teenagers, Eldon decided. *I can even say hello.*

He began to raise his hand in greeting but halted, shyness prevailing, and stuffed it back in his pocket instead.

What would he have said after hello? While he kept strolling down the sidewalk, he considered his options.

"Happy Halloween," he whispered. That was sufficient. If he passed someone else, he'd say that.

He lifted his head to be on the lookout and felt the first drops of rain hit his forehead.

Eldon pressed on despite the downpour that assaulted the pavement and caused the trees to bend in the strong breeze. In the distance, lightning cut through the darkening sky.

Instinctively, he wrapped his arms around himself, though somehow, the cold didn't bother him. The farther he walked, the less the elements seemed to affect him. He could barely feel the rain against his skin.

An elastic sensation of dread expanded inside him. He was thinking about those black streaks on the siding. How long had those lights been flickering? Something told him he had ignored them for longer than he should have.

Eldon stood in the middle of the sidewalk, peering at the groups of children passing him, umbrellas held above them, shielding their costumes and candies. He saw princesses, vampires, and mummies. Taller figures wore black cloaks and scary masks, characters he couldn't identify.

Then he heard three voices he recognized coming out of the gloaming.

"We can hang out at Mr. King's until the storm passes!" a young boy said.

"Let's go! He's got a haunted house in his garage!" the other boy chimed in.

The small girl in the center shook her blonde head. Her costume looked more like a poncho with a hood, a ghost face adorning the front. Her two companions—maybe the McAllister boys—were also dressed as ghosts, but their white sheets covered their whole heads.

"Happy Halloween!" Eldon said as they ran past him, but they didn't answer.

Gradually, he became aware of an engine sound thrumming beside him. He turned his head toward the street where a red pickup truck stayed even with his stride. Eldon walked faster, and the vehicle matched his pace. When he slowed, the truck did too. Finally, the driver rolled down his window. It was a face he didn't recognize, but the unfamiliar man gave him a friendly smile that put him at ease instantly.

"Need a ride?" the driver asked. "Nasty weather out there." He came to a stop and beckoned for Eldon to approach.

"Sure thing," Eldon answered, drawn to the man. He climbed right into the passenger seat of the pickup without hesitation.

"Hello!" he said as he closed the door. "Thank you for the ride."

"Of course." The truck picked up speed incrementally.

"I'm Eldon Greenfield."

"I'm Ra—er, Ralph," the driver replied.

"Pleasure to meet you." He paused. "Happy Halloween."

Ralph chuckled. "Indeed."

"You live in the neighborhood, I take it?" Eldon asked, proud that he had so much to say.

"We're all neighbors in a way, aren't we?" Ralph turned his face toward him while keeping his eyes on the road. A soft glow surrounded his eyes, his cheeks, and the top of his head, as if a lightbulb hung just above him. Eldon was mesmerized.

"I—lightbulbs," he finally spoke. "I was on my way to the hardware store to get lightbulbs."

"I'll take you where you need to go." Ralph smiled, and the sight dazzled Eldon.

Through his sudden stupor, he felt the truck moving faster, beginning to tip back against an incline, only he couldn't see any hill ahead. There was an illusion of the vehicle lifting into the air, but that was absurd—wasn't it?

And then Eldon remembered what he'd forgotten. He looked at Ralph, bathed in luminosity. He understood now.

"After Nellie died, I had an electrical fire," Eldon said. "I didn't make it out, did I?"

Instead of replying, Ralph steered the car higher. The rain at this level of atmosphere fell more like a light mist, and the clouds parted.

"What did you say your name was?" Eldon asked.

"Raziel," he answered.

"You know something, Raziel? I've spent a long time staying apart from other people. Seems kind of fitting that the day I finally decide I might want something to do with them after all is the same day I'm taken away like this."

"That isn't a coincidence, you must know," Raziel said in a dulcet tone. "It was by design. Seeking out human companionship was your final earthly task. You've been in an in-between place, but it seems you've earned some rest now at last. Nellie will be so pleased. And Marianne."

"M-My mother?" Eldon asked, in awe.

"She can't wait to meet you."

Stunned, he gazed out the window as they climbed higher and higher. A warmth settled into the pit of his stomach, the same feeling he used to get after eating some of his wife's tomato soup.

"Well, I'll be," he said, and Eldon Greenfield ascended into the night sky, now cloudless and lit softly by starlight.

7. Five Years Gone
By Marinda K Dennis

The dog barks loudly out my window. The squirrels must be teasing her again. I squeeze my eyes against the morning sun. My love wraps his arms around me pulling me closer to him.

"Morning, beautiful." A tender kiss on my cheek spreads warmth clear through me.

The alarm clock sounds. I roll over and reach to turn it off, reluctant to answer its call.

I turn back to curl up with him, but only his pillow remains. I pull it in close trying to catch his scent five years gone. A tear escapes landing where his head once lay.

8. The Balland's End
By Marymartha Bell

Why am I here? I never expected to be. I guess, in part, it is because I never cared if I died. I counted myself as already dead, and this is why I am still here. Death is no threat. Pain, discomfort — just inconvenient. Damned, unavoidable, and inconvenient, but just *there*. Growing old is not for cowards... Who would have believed I would *survive* to grow old? Certainly not me. I thought I would always be *already dead*, yet I am *living*... and old.

Always pain now. Always inconvenient. That's normal. But in these times, my spirit is divinely alive.

I roll gingerly onto my side, easing past the sharp edge stabbing from the base of my back through my side as I re-arrange my weight and pull up the crochet blanket my wife made. The wife is always trying to feed me, trying to keep my weight up. Very sweet.

At the thought of her, I return to the now: fragrant breeze blowing in the window, augmented with the sound of kids on their bikes making plans; her voice coming from the kitchen, blending with the song on the stereo where I am playing slide guitar. I never realized the love of a woman could be so good. Even that goofy dog is like a person to me. I never knew the love of family before. Not like this, where all is relaxed, easy, no deviousness or need to be on guard.

The kids have no clue what it was like, hunkering down in the jungle, watching for snakes; or tunnel-ratting for the North Vietcong—climbing through dank muddy holes, in their territory, in the dark, with the smell of men's blood mingling with the stench of cooking cabbage to gag you, just to try to catch a Gook and stab him before he stabbed you. So many good men died. I didn't even know then that the North Vietnamese, the Vietcong, were men—they were just Gooks to me then—but they died too. Their deaths, and the deaths of my friends, left me 'already dead,' though my life went on. I hope the kids never have to *really* know.

I had an odd experience this morning, and it still lingers with me: I woke feeling like I just got back from... somewhere. It must have been a dream.

I am in a military bunker—must be in the States, because it is clean and quiet, but has that military stink to it: leather, old wood, and fresh paint—the blank walls are a blue-gray, and there are wooden folding chairs lining one side of the hallway. I'm sitting on one of these wondering what I'm doing here when two armed corporals come walking down the hall dressed in full battle cammis with rifles drawn.

"What is this about," I demand.

"Come with us, Sir," one says.

I stand—for the first time notice I am in cammis but would be cited for being out of uniform if it was inspection—my black tee not to code, and I've got on my cowboy boots and Stetson. I allow them to herd me down the hallway, protesting: "I deserve to know why I'm here. What? You boys got orders to be dumb?"

"This way, Sir," is all they reply.

They lead me down more echoing empty hallways to a small windowless room with a heavy metal door completely clear of personal clutter with only a small desk, a chair, and a row of file cabinets.

"Your assignment, Sir, is to shred all the files in these cabinets," the

young man explains. *"When you complete that, we'll be back for you. Wait here for us."*

They turn sharply and are gone, the heavy door closing firmly behind them. I notice for the first time a paper shredder and a box of plastic garbage bags on the floor beside the desk. I shrug. Odd. But complying with the assignment seems the fastest way out of this confusing situation, so I get on it.

There are records, forms, and reports in the filing cabinets. I shred and fill the bags, setting the file-folders in a stack. I think that I looked at some of them, but afterward, when I try to recall it, the image is lost to me.

This goes on for a long while, the paper shredder humming and the bags filling, until there is a line of plastic bags in a row against the wall. There are no plastic bags left in the box when I stuff a stack of file-folders into the last half-full bag and tie the top shut.

As I sling the bag into the line with the others, the door swings open. It is the same two guys, but now they're in civvies and unarmed. Yet they still maintain military formality in their blank faces and mannerism. *"Come this way, please, Sir."*

I ask again what this is all about and get the same response. *"This way, Sir."*

A full door, metal hatch style and painted green, swings open; daylight pours in.

"Thank you, Sir," one of them breaks a smile as I go out.

"Yeah..." I am confused, but I nod and give a sloppy salute.

I turn my back to them and face the stark contrast of an early summer, a sunlit day with just a hint of a sweet breeze blowing. At a wooden picnic table under a large oak tree, sits a couple of Marines: Mark and Denny. They are smiling and have been chatting. Both get up to greet me. We shake hands, slap backs. No questions are asked. It seems perfectly natural that they should be here.

"So what is this all about?" I ask once we're all seated at the table.

"Waiting for the bus," Denny smiles. *"Going home!"*

"Cool!—Knew it would come eventually!" I reply. *"But... what was that bit inside all about? Did you guys have to do that too?"*

"Yup," replies Mark, *"It's just gettin' the junk, outta the trunk!"*

I shake my head still confused.

"Been waiting long?" I ask.

They look at each other with a knowing smile, and I feel like I'm outside of some secret joke as a bus pulls up beside us.

I sit up in bed, and Mary is there with her long gray-brown braid sitting over her shoulder and two coffee cups in hand.

"Well good morning, my favorite cowboy." She's smiling. "Look at you just jumping up like that!" I've been sluggish in the mornings since the Parkinsons and COPD took hold. "Did I wake you while I was in the kitchen?" she asks.

"No... The strangest thing just happened to me!" The feeling of confusion is still with me, and I think how crazy this will sound, "I... I guess it was a dream."

"Tell me," she says, sitting on the edge of the bed beside me and sipping coffee.

I know it is 2018... I am in Idaho... and 1968, Vietnam and Cambodia are gone now... They still exist somewhere, but are no more potent in my heart than a newspaper story of something that happened far away... They are sad pieces of history.

Life goes on in a pleasant flow of time with Mary, TV movies, a goofy dog, and naps. Since I cannot play my guitar anymore due to the shakes, I have a sense of frustration at not being able to *do* much; and as time passes, I am progressively weaker. I got down to eighty-nine pounds last winter when I had pneumonia. I never regained my strength, even when I put on thirty pounds. The inactivity is not as hard to bear as it would have been when I was younger.

One quiet New Year's Eve Day, I cuddle up and go to sleep. To do so sounds like the perfect treasure. I just need to rest for a bit...

I open my eyes, and I am gazing directly into the eyes of Granma Bell. I do not question this. It seems so natural. The last thing I can remember happening was holding Mary, then getting on my horse's back and riding out onto a flat with a few aspens toward the pine-covered foothills. It looked like the

Tetons… When did that happen?

I gaze contentedly into the eyes of love and adoration, inches from me. I realize Granma is holding me, all of me, in both arms, swaying, and singing quietly in Lakota. I wish for nothing but am at total rest, perfect contentment. Gradually I become aware of the strands of her straight hair, deep blue-black, that hang down and dance in the gentle breeze, reflecting muted sunlight in bright contrast, brushing against her soft smooth neck. I could stay here forever.

She lays me down. It is a soft bed, smelling of wicker basket and the woods. That scent forms words in my mind for the first time since waking: "Smells like home…. I must be home." I have a sense of awe and wonderment. The question is not fully formed, but the thought is present *How did I get here?*

I stand up. I do this without thinking; I just stand. Instinctively I look down at my body. The question arises into my consciousness: *How did I get here?… Who am I?* I see myself. I am small and smooth skinned with hard muscles, thin and limber. I look around and see that Granma is nowhere near, but I sense that she is well. My thoughts shift to Mark, and a mischievous boyhood grin spreads across my face. I run down the porch toward the woods, shouting, "Mark! Mark!"

My mouth gets still as my feet move silently. I can hear my rapid, strong breathing. My feet know the way. Down the familiar trail toward the treehouse, past the trees I know, the smell of the big funguses growing there, the blue flax blooming in a patch of radiant green grass near the base of the sycamore on this beautiful late spring morning. I run up the tree into our treehouse and put my head inside the doorway. Mark is sitting on his bed, leaning against the wall, whittle stick and pocketknife in hand, grinning.

"Well, you took long enough to get here!" he says.

We're jumping and hugging, slapping each other's backs and "whoo-hoo"-ing. Delight is seeping through me. I am fully alive.

"Com'mon," he says. And without a plan we take off down the tree and onto the trail toward the river.

I am breathing in the Ozarks. We are standing silently on the bank of the river listening to it flow, listening to the wind in the trees, the birds in the branches tweeting and chattering to each other. Far overhead a hawk is floating like a silhouette against the wispy clouds in a soft blue sky. I watch it catch the current and turn. It is calling to me. *How is it calling?* And in an instant, I am the hawk. I feel the wind beneath my wings instinctively knowing how to press against the current to rise or dip. The delight is vibrating through me, and I am fully alive!

I float with the currents, undirected, just flying; and somehow this seems perfectly natural, perfectly normal, though fully invigorating. I am rapt, relaxed, engaged. The countryside below me is at once familiar and yet new. I follow the course of the river as it meanders through the mountain valleys.

I see a gathering of people there, in a clearing of trees near the river; perhaps a family reunion. There are so many. Clearly a picnic with tables spread and chairs arranged. My curiosity overwhelms me; and, without any attention to the mechanics of flight, I move in closer. That inattention to logistics catches my notice, and I dip upward for just a movement, observing that the sky is still clear and wide open around me. I could fly off, but the attraction of the gathering pulls at me, gently coaxing me to come... It is the gaze of a familiar friend... Mark stands watching me with his hands on his hips as I touch down smiling.

I feel the ground under my feet, and I am standing. A quick glance shows me my most familiar body: twenties? thirties? forties? I am thin, powerful, stout and resilient. Mark is in his ageless body of "adult" now and stands close, gazing hard at me, still smiling. "Good to see you, Brother," says he. "Nice entrance."

"Good to be here," says I—*wherever 'here' is.*

Pops walks up, his glossy black hair shining in the sun, his face covered in a joyful grin. He puts his arms around me and rocks. "My boy! My boy!" he chants, just as he did when I was a child.

"I love you Pops," says I, to my surprise. I have never spoken these words before.

"I love you, my Sun-Cloud, my Bobby," he says, calling me by my Native name—he has never spoken these words before either, never acknowledge my Lakota roots, and never spoken the love I have always known he has for me.

From within the embrace with Pops, I notice Granma Bell—Mary Inez—standing with ... could it be? Is that Mamie Jewel Midkiff—Granma Juanita? Perhaps it had been, but... very different. She is young and is wearing what looks like a deerskin dress and Cherokee headband. Is that Pop—John—Tonkoff?

And another, even more familiar person... Though I have never before seen him, I know him full well. He appears tall with dark hair shining brightly. He gazes intently at me, smiling in a warmth that radiates from across the lawn. I know he is enjoying watching me greet my best loves from throughout my lifetime. He does not greet me, for he has been with me all along.

I close my eyes and am easy in the sustained embrace with Pops, the feel of the breeze on my face, the bubbling of the river, the voices of laughter. The music starts. A harmonica sounds. Other instruments join in playing rifts and tuning: guitars, mandolins, and fiddles. Pops and I step back from our embrace, and the strength of his gaze and smile fills me.

I am... *here*... it is *Now*... I am alive, fully alive... I was dead, but now I am here... I am here, it is Now, and I am alive.

Mary is lying next to me, smiling at me, petting my hair. I am smiling at her from somewhere else in the room somewhere above her. A tear rolls down her cheek. "Oh Baby," she places her hand on my leaden still chest. "That was beautiful. You sure tell a good story." She closes her eyes and tenderly kisses my forehead goodbye.

9. Hamewith and Hairsair
A Prose Poem
By T Antoff

Author's Note: This work incorporates both Scots and English, often entangled and intermingled. For ease of comprehension, and with many thanks to Fiona Roberston for consultation and support, I have included a glossary of words and terms at the conclusion.

Part 1: Hame

Your haar filled my lungs with saltwater.

You were the first full breath I took. And each breath after.

As I stole and wound with veins and blood, you stole with me. Through cobblestoned streets and past the dead in the kirkyard, beside the ghosts of rebellions and feral goats. You lit fires and painted my cheeks with ash. You bared pendulums like breasts and beggar's pouches to the beat of drums, blessed us by all the fucking that ever was tucked in among the hills. You were transgression and magnificence.

You led processions through the streets by torchlight, bled into ink on ancient pages cracking without cotton glove, spat in the heart of Midlothian to join all the bile of before and all the strangers' kisses of now. You cemented steps into the sea and built your castles on cliffs from sandstone to fill with paw prints and Buckfast. You were oil-made rich. Oil-made poor, eroded by Oxfords and Wellies and turned into waste for the grouse and the gun.

Aye. You *are*.

Only I am not with you. I am outwith home.

Hamewith is aye ahent me. A'm aye backwart without ye.

Part 2: Hairtsair

I cannot allow myself to remember the feel of him, nestling against my chest, breathing lightning into my neck, attempting to suckle with teeth. Instead, I've inked him in, pinned him with needles and hoped that they would go deep enough to scar. I wanted to feel him when I ran my fingertips across the muscles cradling my soft throat, but now I only have glimpses in the mirror and images trapped in screens that I can't bring myself to look at. My reflection flickers as it always does, and he is not there.

I want to give up mourning for celebration.

I want to.

But he was the loss in the middle that broke me when I thought myself already broken. First home. Then one. Then another. Then him. Another to follow.

I blamed the loss of the first for the cancer that took him, swelling his throat and pinching his breath, lacing through muscle and vein and sinew so thoroughly that there was no excising it, making me choose between keeping him for a few more days and letting him go while he still thought himself well.

I had so much to blame. The dank and deadly muck climbing the corners of the walls. The mice that scurried over our feet. The cold in the uninsulated front room. The chemicals they sprayed to get rid of the biting bugs that they assured us was a fine, safe poison, as safe as any poison could be. Muck and mice, a pleasant poison, but above all, myself.

My inability to protect him. My inability to keep him safe. My inability to keep us all home.

We were so far away.

And so far from home, I remembered what it was like to be too terrified to move, to smoke on the porch, to go out the backdoor at night. I remembered what it was like to stand utterly still while foundations cracked and threatened. I remembered what it was like to know that they were gunshots instead of fireworks.

I left my spirit behind in the leaving—a move they called it—and I blamed myself for all the cancers that took its place.

Entr'acte: On water

I'd always lived near water. Close enough —but never close enough—to the ocean, or the bay, or the sea. As a child I went wild swimming in lakes and rivers, and once in the flooded field behind my house. I grew up in a swamp, albeit one that had been swallowed by concrete suburbs and shopping malls, retaining little of the marsh that birthed us beyond basements that filled with water and mosquitoes. When I came home, it was to water.

From my bed in the first place I lived once I went home but before I called it that, I could be at the river in seconds and follow it two miles to the sea.

So, let me tell you of the sea. Of the rivers. Of the firths. Of burns and falls and devil's pulpit.

Let me tell you of the water.

Her boons come with storms to blend day with night, her beauty with the waterlogged wool of some fisherman's guernsey stitched so that his body could find its way home.

She gives favors of sand and mud and peat, offers us glistening, slippery stones, glass softened enough to run fingers along edges. Snakes and eels to create waves like ribbons. Seals to twirl as though idle, creating current around them. Tadpoles to be scooped in bare hands while the indifferent eyes of parents watch. Jellyfish to sting thighs like graceful savagery made giggly, until the tide brings them shimmering to dry on the shore. Fish to dart and bite and dance beneath the water, to leap above, a frenzy of fin and scale.

She gives us inwart, outwart, while we jump her waves until breathless and still breathing.

Gies a bosie, giftit then taken away. And she does not love us.

But it does not matter.

She gave us life and flesh and pudgy depth. Abandoned in dependence, we became husks who needed to swallow her deep to feel, to forget, to sleep. When we walked away from her, we carried her liquid with us, took it to keep us warm, to be able to smile easily, to feel connected. Her within us. Her, fermented and distilled, fire from the water. As all things are from the water. Filling our stomach as she filled our blood, racing through our meat and mind, and marking us as dull as we are radiant.

When we stood on her shores and watched her rising tide, her rain-swelled belly, she threatened and enticed: *Come closer and I will rip you away. Come closer and I will make you buoyant, lighter than you thought possible. I will let you fly. I will teach you how to drown. I'll show you life free within me. I'll cast it rotten at your feet. I'll turn play into terror. Work into companionship. I'll feed you. Starve you. Come closer.*

She holds our ghosts within her bosom, and I came. To play. To ponder. To sit and let myself feel my place as though it were comfort. I've sucked water—clear and trickling down from the hills—off my fingers without care for whatever it carried with it. I've swum naked. I've hid my unhappy body in layers that the swimming would turn sheer and sticky. I've fucked in water. Cried in water. Once, twice, thrice, decided that I would go in water.

I've given to water. And lost to water. Over and over again.

But I am not alone in this. None of us are. We could not be.

We've all come from. All left. All lost. All given.

We will always entwine in this. With her.

Part 3: Hame

You were hills I couldn't climb and all the spaces where I wandered. Lowlands and highlands and Pentlands. Bullers and bay. Cleuch and glen and me even-paced but uneven-gaited. You were all those who would walk for me, run for me, bring me water from your peaks along with trembling grasses that grew nowhere else.

You were the full moon rising south, peeking over, climbing higher. You were the fox on his three-a.m.-rounds beneath her, marking each tree, clockwork in footsteps and musk, red and white and black. You were the smoke trickling from my lips and merging with the mist of the morn. You were the spiderwebs turned to lace with frost.

You were beloved gorse.

When I left you, I wanted to fill my hillside with your weeds. I wanted those thorns that sprouted from any crack and stretched up into yellow to dim the sun. I wanted your ferocity and tenaciousness. I wanted to extend a brown finger like your branches to the powers that stripped me from you and watch it sprout like glorious fungus, one finger then two. I wanted to show them the beauty of your decay, the glory of nae giein a fuck.

I wanted to remember in a way that felt like living. I wanted my right to roam and to strip layer from layer in 16 degrees, giving the gift of sweat and bliss with a face turned to the sky and collecting mist. I wanted to remember your dead. Blackhouses. Rebellions. I wanted to remember your sheep gates and cairns. The prayers that were offered. The longings that were mine and not mine all at once.

I wanted to remember the snails and the slugs.

~

I miss the slugs. Not the ones that would burst under our feet, caught between concrete and careless shoe. Not the ones I had to pry from my dog's sticky jowls after my partner threw bread into the garden for the birds in the morning. But the slugs, nonetheless. The ones who would leave vines of glitter across every steppingstone and broken brick. The ones who would pop pop their eyes towards me and away. The one I rescued from the cat who had found its way beneath the door and to the bowl of food as if it could swim in a sea of grain free kibble and come away from it ready to take on the magpies waiting just outside.

I miss their black and opalescent backs amid moss that would suck at my ankles. Our buckets full so that we could carry them away from our herbs and veg, give them safe wild places and the crumbling church by the Don. Theys in all their boneless glory, heads peeking out, gliding so slowly away.

~

I'd never thought home could be a place. Strange that. Home is where the heart is, they say. But the heart is flesh, in flesh, and so home was flesh, in flesh. In mine. In others. Heart isn't something you tear in half or bitty pieces and give away. It beats from within, and so I'd always thought it remained within. Perhaps that is what's intended. It's metaphor, symbol. But I like them to be consistent.

Tell me then, can you live without a heart? If home is where the heart is, and home is so far away that I can no longer feel it beating, am I still alive?

Part 4: Hairtsair

I still cannot speak of ghosts without conjuring them, forming rivulets turned to waterfalls that bore caverns into my chest.

Did you know that I couldn't hold him when he died?

And that I don't regret it? The pool beneath my ribs was already overflowing with him.

You were named after a ghost who was haunting my time; and yet, now that you are gone, it is neither him nor you who haunts me. Peaceful and knowing that you were loved, you have passed, leaving me the ghost with no tether, ever haunted and ever haunting. Now I am someone else's endless wandering in the hopes of feeling you again.

I want you back. Every day, every hour, with every

heartbeat in my ghostly chest I want you back. And yet I cannot, will not, pull you away from your peace to wander with me. My epitaph reads only for you: *Opre opre: My loves, someday, I will rejoin you.*

Entr'acte: On Grief

People talk of grief as though it were something that settles on you and becomes stagnant. But it is vibrant, vicious, living.

Grief becomes blood, becomes body, becomes the sun ever rising ever falling, hanging at a remembered eye level, cold and grey. It is not so much something to wade through until you reach dry land as it is something that shifts the ground permanently beneath you, leaving you only a misstep from going under. It's the ghosts that save us, wrapping ethereal fingers around our forearms, reminding that our hearts still beat, steadying us when we stumble. As we move ever forward, they become our companions. As much harbingers of the future as reminders of the past, and blurring the lines between each and our present. They recast our memories into light and dark, lighter and darker. They bring as many tears of loss as tears of joy and once having. They push us towards. Our ghosts are blessings. Sturdy despite their incorporeality. They collect us as we collect them, building fortresses of the gone from scavenged pasts, shoring us against all the futures that could be.

Sometimes I feel as though I have too many ghosts, and yet, they are not the ones who break me. I am. Pinned with desire for more, for longer with, for time that I couldn't hold onto. The ghosts are not steel, not sharp and piercing. They remind me to move. To seize. To mourn and become better for it. Aches exist to remind us of our body, of our spirit, of our love.

Part 5: Hame

You were.

Aye, only I am no with you. Hamewith is ever before me, ever behind me. All that I am is backwards now.

You were.

You were the mercat cross that knew the cost of bodies. You were the gulls swimming overhead. The nipped fingers, stumbling feet, oh-too-loud voices of tourists. The bleating of young tipped from safe nests. The hollowed streets and hallowed midnight dawn. You were the rocks beyond the windows streaming ever north, south, ever west, ever east. You were rigs glistening between above and below, the helicopters like clockworks. You were the winds and the waves. You were pillboxes on Balgownie, Junes on Balmedie.

You were all those who threw themselves from monuments and bridges, and all those who will. Ostentatious and quiet, one to skid traffic to a halt, the other to drift alone and unfound for days. You were all the people breaking their bodies on concrete, on water, on the fists of those who claimed to love them. You were all the people who broke their necks protesting and praying. You were the castle on the dragon's back, fierce and deadly, even when you swore to protect.

I want those lonely moments on the steps in Obar Dheathain, watching her swallow deep enough to lap at my toes and knowing at least this time she will retreat. I want the Forth's firth and its siren's call. I want An t-Eilean Skye and the sea at my doorstep and the first place that I ever holidayed that I wished to call home. I want backwards, more and more again. I want the sand crabs of my youth scurrying to burrow through my fingers, the horseshoes my father would once take me yearly to see. I want pools and snails. The leech on my palm. I want the North Sea biting my skin. I want the silence of my heartbeat, floating, so wet that I can no longer tell water from air. I want the slap of my palm in the tub learning the feeling of surface tension, learning the magic of air trapped within glass, learning to love and to wonder and to awe. I want the rain that comes like mist sideways, drenching deeper than bone. I want the wind and thunder that shakes the house, that reminds us she can bring us down or lift us up. I want wellies and skipping to rescue worms when I still thought myself capable of rescuing anything.

I want my grandmother, my wee one. I want what I've lost. I want to go home.

Part 6: Hairtsair

Once upon a time I used to feed him pomegranate seeds. One for you, a handful for me. Once upon a time, he would wait patiently for slices of green pepper, gnaw happily on kiwi skins, puncture peaches like a vampire fruitarian and then leave them abandoned to soften and ferment. Once upon a time my wee loon walked the world like it belonged to him. Once upon a time it did. His world, from one door to the next, the winter sun streaming through our lounge door, brick throwers and get tae fuck from the other. Now the world belongs to no one but those gone from it.

If home is in all the others, in all the loves we've lost and are yet to, in all the places my ragged heart has gone, where does it go when they do? Where is it now? Have they taken it with them?

If so, part of it is ash, sitting on the shelf above my television, next to the virgin and the strumpet.

Part of it has been cast to the sea.

Finale: Outwith and Hamewart

When we left home it was above and across the water, blinded by the sun. Burning light in sea and river, reflected in snow and ice. Water-hewn craigs, careful old wounds and blazing new, in-filled with light.

It is good, I think.

Leaving home should blind, should burn, should set alight the fields and the moors and the hills, and everything that had settled so deep within me that I do not know how to breathe without tasting them. Lost and hanging between land and sky, I wished for incineration to lay bare and make anew. I wished for smoke to coat lung and throat like peat flame, fog and sea spray, so that, upon waking, I could never forget the fire that once burned within.

Only through the leaving to come home again.

A'm only leaving to come hame again.
Outwith, aye, a'm hamewart ageen.

Additional note on Scots:

Scots is a language with a long and extensive history, sharing a common ancestor with English, but not derived from it. Its recent past has seen attempts to diminish or dismiss it, to erase or eradicate it; however, it has persisted. It is a language with a vibrant history, present, and future and has always been a language of politics and literature, culture and community. It is ever-living, ever-evolving.

For ease of comprehension the glossary follows. I will be the first to say that these definitions are not complete; they are shaped by and limited to the ways I made use of these words and phrases specifically within this piece.

Glossary:

A'm: I am

Ageen: again

Ahent: 'behind', but in the sense of 'left behind', in the past

An t-Eilean Skye: an island in the Inner Hebrides; a hybrid of the Gaelic 'an t-Eilean' (the island) and the English place name of 'Skye'

Aye: 'yes' or 'always'

Backwart: backward, both in the sense of direction and indicating ignorance

Burn: a stream, from a small watercourse you can step across to a near-river

Cairn: a marker made of piled stones.

Cleuch: a ravine with steep sides, usually cut by a burn

Firth: a river inlet where it meets the sea

Get tae fuck: go away, similar to 'fuck off' but with more scorn and derision

Gies a bosie: gives a hug or 'give me a hug'

Giftit: given as a gift

Gorse: a large, thorny, flowering shrub that can grow almost anywhere

Haar: a dense and heavy, though often swirling, sea fog

Hairtsair: heartsore; a kind of sadness which includes longing and loss

Hame: home, both in place and in meaning

Hamewith: homewards, more in the sense of looking towards home

Hamewart: homewards, more in the sense of heading towards home

Inwart: movement inwards

Kirkyard: a churchyard, usually a cemetery

Loon: a young man, usually used to describe healthy, sometimes irresponsible young men

Mercat: a gathering place where, traditionally, markets were held

Nae giein a fuck: not giving a fuck

Obar Dheathain: Gaelic name for Aberdeen

Outwart: heading outwards, moving away from something

Outwith: outside, out of, beyond

Wee: small, often used affectionately

Wellies: or Wellingtons; rubber or polyurethane, waterproof boots

Ye: you

10. Spell Casters
By Loriane Parker

*To my mother, Laural Diane Parker, who shared
with me the magic and beauty of language.*

My mother stopped the car in front of a house with a "For Sale" sign in the front yard. The yellow color of the two-storey colonial reminded me of sunflowers. In front of the house, a winding path led through a garden of flowers, towering oak trees, and a large Japanese maple with soft, feathery branches. The front door, made of red oak, had an oval-shaped leaded-glass window in the center. If there was such a thing as a happy house, this was it. Mom and I smiled.

"It's perfect," we both said.

Inside, sunlight streamed through the windows to shine on the polished hardwood floors. We walked past the fireplace in the family room and into the kitchen with its floor-to-ceiling white cabinets and gray granite countertops.

"It's beautiful!" Mom said. "It's just like the kitchens on TV!"

"It is beautiful," I agreed.

A slender, middle-aged woman approached us. Her strong

perfume enveloped us as she handed us a flyer. Her perfectly manicured fingernails were painted a bright shade of red.

"Welcome!" She said with exuberance. She introduced herself as the realtor in charge of selling the house. She pointed out various features of the home that were listed on the flyer. She didn't speak to me, just Mom. "Are you looking to buy?"

"Yes, we are," Mom said. She mentioned she was a writer and a middle school English teacher.

"Wonderful! Are you from the area?"

"Yes. We've lived in Chesterfield for a long time."

"Does your daughter go to Parkway Central?" The realtor smiled at me.

High school. I refrained from rolling my eyes. I was thirty-four years old, but I was very petite; and when I was with Mom, people often mistook me for a teenager. It was awkward to correct them. I had never planned to be living with my mom at my age, but my car accident had changed everything. At least my settlement had made it possible for us to finally afford something we had always wanted: a family home.

"She graduated from Parkway West." Mom said. She put her arm around my shoulders and hugged me. "We'd like to take a look around."

"Of course," the realtor said. "Let me know if you have any questions."

"Thank you."

Mom and I toured the backyard and pool, the upstairs bedrooms, and the finished basement with a wine cellar.

"What do you think?" Mom asked.

"I love it," I said. "It feels like home. I want to buy it."

"Me too."

We stopped at the formal living room.

"We don't need a formal living room," Mom said. "What would we use this room for? Maybe a sitting room?"

"Let's make it a library!"

"Oh! Our own library!"

As we stood there in the large, square room, we envisioned tall shelves of books, art prints, maybe a tapestry.

Mom took out her cell phone. "I'll call Brenda."

Our realtor.

A month later we moved in, along with my younger sister Mary, who was going back to college to change careers. We enjoyed decorating the home together as a family, picking out paint colors for the rooms, hanging pictures.

We all loved the library. We lined two of the walls with floor-to-ceiling bookshelves. We chose red-and-gold brocade fabric for the chairs and loveseat. On the round wood table, we put a fancy chess set, modeled after the one in the movie version of *Harry Potter and the Sorcerer's Stone*. Art prints of dragons and faeries and a tapestry hung on the walls. Heavy drapes framed the tall windows. Next to Mom's favorite chair was a wooden side table, its stand carved in the shape of an elephant—Mom's favorite animal. The lampshades were edged with beaded fringe. Books of every subject filled the shelves: fiction and non-fiction, history and philosophy, poetry, short stories, novels, and biographies. There were over-sized art books and picture books, leather-bound hard covers and soft-cover paperbacks. Each book contained an adventure waiting to be discovered.

The day we finished decorating the library, Mom and I stood back and admired it.

"Books are magic," I said.

"Yes," Mom said. "As writers, we get to create that magic. We cast spells on our readers to bring them beauty and enjoyment."

I had never thought about that before. Mom was such a talented writer. She was a great storyteller—a true spell caster. I hoped I'd be as good a storyteller as she was someday.

Over the next several years, we added more treasures to the library: an hourglass, a small bust of Nefertiti, an end table with more shelves that we quickly filled up with books. Mom and I often discussed the different books we were reading, and the stories we were each writing. The library continued to evolve, taking on a life and a magic all its own.

On her sixty-fifth birthday, Mom sat in her favorite chair, her feet resting on a large, tufted ottoman. Our two Corgis, Vicki and Phoebe, curled up nearby, taking a nap on the Persian rug. The soft lamplight glinted off Mom's wire-rimmed glasses. With her chin-length haircut, she looked like she'd just stepped out of a Mary Englebright illustration. She proudly showed me her hardcover copy of Beowulf, translated by one of her favorite writers, Seamus Heaney.

"I love Old English," she said. "It has such visual, evocative words for things. A skeleton is called a *'bonecage.'*" She grinned. "Isn't that wonderful?"

That was last year, before her colon cancer.

For ten months, she suffered. At times her pain was unbearable. Her body struggled to fight the cancer, and she gradually withered away. It was the first time she had looked old. Her spirit dimmed; her smile vanished. The pain medications made her so drowsy that when she was awake, she just stared into the distance. We couldn't talk to each other anymore. She stopped telling her stories. She struggled to read a few books. In a way, I lost her before she died. When she passed away the day before Halloween, I felt as though a part of me had been ripped out, leaving behind a gaping emptiness.

She was gone for several days before I could bring myself to enter the library. I couldn't bear her absence. I wanted her back. In the dark, silent room, I stared at her empty chair. Her Seamus Heaney *Beowulf* lay on the elephant table, a bookmark placed between the pages. She had been re-reading it recently. It had always been one of her favorites. I couldn't bear to place it back on the shelf; she would never pick it up again.

Without Mom, the house no longer brought me joy. All I saw were empty places where she should be. It was supposed to be *our* home, *our* library; and now, she was gone.

The week before Christmas, my sister Mary and I wrapped

presents for the dogs. We didn't have kids, so the dogs were our fur babies. If we opened presents on Christmas and didn't give them any, they would feel left out and get upset.

Plush squeaky dog toys are oddly shaped and rather challenging to wrap. I chose gift wrap with candy canes printed on it. I rolled up a plush squeaky mouse and folded the paper on the ends to cover the toy as best I could. During the process, I accidentally pushed on the mouse, and it squeaked loudly in response. Vicki barked from the kitchen. Mary and I laughed.

"I wish Mom could be here to see the pups play with their presents," I said.

"Me too." Mary said. She sat next to me at the dining room table, which was covered with bows and rolls of wrapping paper. "It was one of her favorite things about Christmas." Mary was four years younger and a few inches taller than I was. The golden highlights in her long, red hair shone in the light from the dining room chandelier. She picked up a roll of giftwrap that had teddy bears printed on it. Somehow, her presents turned out looking much neater than mine did. She picked up a pen and wrote "PHOEBE" on the present she'd just wrapped.

I wrote VICKI on the present I'd just finished wrapping. We wrapped a few more toys for each pup; then we carried the presents to the family room and tucked them under the tree with our own gifts. Vicki and Phoebe followed us. Their pointed ears stood straight up as they eagerly sniffed the presents.

"These are for Christmas," Mary said.

They left the wrapped treasures alone. We'd had the pups for several years, and we would put their presents under the tree every year. The pups never took anything unless we handed it to them. We could set a plate with a steak on it on the coffee table, well within their reach, and they wouldn't touch it. They were such good dogs.

The next day, when Mary was at work, I went upstairs to my room and turned on my computer. I loved writing short stories and novels, but it was hard for me to write. In my car accident, I suffered catastrophic abdominal injuries and brain damage. Chronic intestinal obstructions and narcolepsy made it impossible for me to keep a regular schedule, so I couldn't work a job. I was home all day, and I didn't feel very well most of the time. Mom had been a huge comfort to me. She had always encouraged me to write. It was my outlet, my way of transforming whatever I was feeling into something beautiful.

"Mom," I said, "thanks for teaching me to write."

I thought it would help me feel a little better to talk to her as though she could hear me, but it didn't. I stared at my blank computer screen, trying to work on one of my stories. Images filled my thoughts, but I couldn't shape them into words. No matter how hard I concentrated, the words wouldn't come. All I managed to do was give myself a headache.

I rested my head in my hands. "I miss you so much, Mom. I wish you were here."

Squeaks sounded from downstairs. Squeaky dog toys.

The dogs had a toy basket filled with their toys, but Mary and I never gave it to them unless we could watch them. They had a habit of pulling out and eating squeakers, prompting several visits to the veterinarian's office. Had I left the toy basket down by accident?

I hurried downstairs and walked toward the family room. The squeaking grew louder, and I heard paws thundering on the carpet as Vicki and Phoebe ran around the room. When I reached the Christmas tree, I stopped.

All the pups' presents had been opened. The torn-up wrapping paper and bows were strewn across the floor. Vicki and Phoebe bounded around the room, squeaking their new toys. They turned and smiled at me. They were having a great time. Each dog was playing only with the toys that Mary and I had picked out for them. How had the pups known which toys were theirs? They hadn't touched my presents, or Mary's. Ours were still wrapped under the tree.

I picked up the phone and called Mary at work. "You'll never guess what happened."

"What?"

"The pups are having Christmas a little early," I said. "While I was upstairs, they opened all their presents. They're playing with their new toys."

"Oh no! Don't let Vicki rip up Phoebe's toys! Vicki destroys everything!"

"Vicki is only playing with her own toys," I said, "and Phoebe's only playing with hers."

Mary and I were both silent for a few moments.

"Really?" Mary asked.

"Yes."

"Wow," Mary said. "Well, I guess you can let them play with them for a little while. Just pick them up before they totally destroy them. I want to watch them play with them when I get home."

"Okay."

I sat in the family room and watched the pups play. Phoebe brought me one of her toys, and I played fetch with her. Vicki lied down and started to rip up one of her toys with her teeth.

After a while, I said, "Okay pups, that's enough for now. We have to make the toys last so Mary can watch you play with them too when she gets home from work."

I picked up the toys and put them on a shelf, then gave each dog a treat. For a few moments I looked around the family room. Phoebe never opened her presents. She always watched with excitement as Mary opened them for her. Vicki would always rip open hers, but only when I handed them to her. She had never pulled any out from under the tree before. And how had each dog gotten all the right gifts? Maybe Mom had opened presents with the pups this year after all.

I shook my head. I wanted that to be true, but I didn't really believe it. I hitched up the pups in their harnesses and leashes and took them out for a walk.

Spring came, and the Magnolia tree in our backyard bloomed, its clusters of flowers raining pink petals down upon the ground. Lilies of the Valley poked their green stems through the mulch, their white, bell-shaped blossoms partly concealed by their stiff leaves. Purple and blue Periwinkle flowers dotted the slender vines that covered the tree roots. On a white trellis nearby, Bourbon roses bloomed a soft shade of pink as they climbed toward the sky. Those roses had been mom's favorite flower. They were bright and had a wonderful fragrance. They also didn't have any thorns. Mom had been just like them, a rose without thorns. All she did was bring beauty into the world. Today was her birthday, the first one that had come since she had passed. I wished she could see our Bourbon roses now.

I wanted to do something to commemorate her on her birthday. I called Vicki and Phoebe over to the Magnolia Tree. With a jar full of dog treats, I coaxed them into sitting right next to each other under the tree, surrounded by pink Magnolia petals scattered across the mulch. They smiled in the way that Corgis do. As the sunlight shone on their thick golden-and-white fur, I took several pictures. I only made them sit for a couple of minutes. "Good girls!" I said. I gave them some treats.

Vicki and Phoebe curled up next to me as I sat on the grass. Nearby, pots of pink Geraniums lined the pool deck, the pool's blue water clear and shimmering in the sun. The Mazus bloomed between the patio stones, filling in the spaces with tiny purple blossoms. Groups of bright red Astilbe, their feathery clusters of flowers shaped like bottle brushes, bloomed between blue Hydrangeas. Purple Meadow Sage framed the pedestal of the bird bath. The lilac bush, so tall it stretched over the top of the cedar fence, swayed back and forth in the breeze. Beneath the towering Tulip tree, large yellow-and-black butterflies fluttered to the trailing lavender by our statue of St. Francis of Assisi. Mom and I had picked out everything in the garden together: each flowering plant, every shrub, the statues, the stones in the patio.

Our oasis, Mom used to call it. It had been my sanctuary. Now it only reminded me that she was gone.

The dogs and I went inside. I washed the dishes in the kitchen sink, watching the butterflies outside, fluttering amongst the flowers.

"It's such a beautiful day, Mom." I couldn't bring myself to smile. "I can't be happy because you're not here. I love you, Mom. I know you can't hear me, but Happy Birthday."

Something swept back my hair as though someone was gathering it back into a ponytail. When I was a little girl, Mom would brush my hair and put it back into a high ponytail for me. I touched the back of my hair. There wasn't a draft. The windows were closed, so they weren't letting in the breeze. "Mom?"

I turned around. There was no one there.

It's just my imagination, I thought. *No matter how much I wish Mom was here, she's gone.*

That afternoon, I sat at my desk and stared at my blank computer screen. I wanted to write so badly. I loved to write sword and sorcery stories. More than ever, I wanted to carry myself away to an imaginary place and focus on my characters' experiences rather than my own. The process of storytelling had always amazed me. I created the setting and the characters, but the characters took on a life of their own. I put them in situations, but they made their own choices. Sometimes, they surprised me. Storytelling was partly something I controlled and partly a journey of discovery. It was a mystery. I missed it. Since my mom had passed away, I had not been able to translate images into written words. I left words out when I wrote sentences; I omitted transitions between paragraphs. Sometimes, I could summarize a scene, but I couldn't write the scene itself. It was bad enough I had lost Mom; I didn't want to lose my writing too. It was one of the most wonderful gifts she had given me.

I pulled out a decorative box from a nearby shelf. The box was colored deep purple with a bright blue lid. I had bought it at a craft store after finding it in the scrapbooking section. It contained a stack of birthday cards that Mom and I had given to each other over the years. This was the first year I couldn't give her a birthday card. I realized it would also be the first year I wouldn't get one from her. I pulled out a card with a picture of violets on the front—my favorite flower. It was the first birthday card she had given me after my car accident. Inside the card, Mom had written, "Happy Birthday, Lori. I'm so glad you lived to see another year."

I hadn't thought about my accident in a while. It was nineteen years ago. I was just twenty-four years old at the time. I was driving home late at night, and the pouring rain splattered on my windshield like a wall of water obscuring my view. I didn't see the other car coming toward me until it was right in front of me. Its headlights were turned off. Then the impact. My femur snapped like a twig. The steering wheel slammed into my abdomen and broke most of my ribs. For a few seconds I felt nothing. Then terrible, terrible pain. Pain exploded through my abdomen and chest and kept getting worse and worse until I couldn't stand it, and I screamed and screamed. Then it was cold. Someone had opened my car door. Flashing lights glinted off shards of broken glass. I wasn't moving, and I wasn't screaming anymore.

At the hospital, people rushed around me. I passed in and out of consciousness. I had the chance to see Mom and Mary and say goodbye to them. Mom looked terrified; Mary was crying. Then I was rushed into surgery. The huge lamp over the operating table switched on. I stared into the bright light until it faded to blackness.

In the dark, my pain stopped. I was aware of a powerful presence that was kind and comforting. I was at peace. I felt something wrapped around me like a cozy blanket. It was love, a love so powerful I could touch it. I could feel it in every part of my being. It was as though I was suspended and supported by love itself. I wasn't in my body, but I wasn't in Heaven yet. I knew I was going to die, but I wasn't afraid. What I didn't know was that I was going to come back. I spent the next several weeks in a coma and had another near-death experience. When I woke up, Mom was there for me to tell her about it.

What if my near-death experiences were just produced by my own brain, and Heaven didn't exist at all? It had been easy to believe when Mom was here.

If anyone belonged in Heaven, Mom did. For almost two decades she comforted me during miserable medical procedures and kept me company when I was in pain. When I came out of every surgery, she was there waiting for me. She was a huge support for me. She was my best friend.

I wiped tears from my face. I went to the library and sat in Mom's favorite chair. Vicki and Phoebe stretched out on the floor, basking in a sunbeam that streamed through the leaded glass window in the front door. I curled up and hugged Mom's copy of *Beowulf* until Mary came home from work.

It took me a while to fall asleep that night. Then something awakened me. I opened my eyes.

Mom sat in the chair in the corner of my room. She wore her comfortable house robe and slippers. She looked the way she had before the cancer: a healthy weight, strong, with good color to her skin. Her chin-length hair was once again thick and soft.

I couldn't move. It was as though time had stopped. I could actually feel her presence, like I could when she was alive. A tear streaked down my face.

Mom smiled. "I'm really here," she said. "You're not dreaming."

I couldn't speak, but a single word formed in my mind: *Stay.*

"Just for a little while," she said. "I was allowed to come back because there's something I'm supposed to tell you. I'm supposed to deliver a message. There's something you're supposed to write about angels and Heaven, and you know what it is."

I blinked, and she was gone.

I was able to move again. I sat up and stared at the empty chair. Vicki jumped up and put her paws on my mattress. I reached down to pet her.

I would sometimes tell people about my near-death

experiences, but I had never written about them. I wrote fantasy fiction, not non-fiction. To write about my own experiences would be something entirely new for me.

The soft blue light of dawn that filled my room brightened with the rising sun. I took Vicki outside, then fixed my morning cup of coffee.

When I turned on my computer and sat down at the keyboard, I glanced over at the empty chair in the corner of the room. Mom wasn't there. Yet somehow, I knew she would always be with me. I turned back to the computer screen. My mind filled with images, not from my imagination, but from my memories. I began to type. For the first time since Mom had died, words finally came to me. I, the spell caster's daughter, would now share with readers a magic of my own.

11. The Music Box
By Christopher Frost

for Michelle Alicia Modica,
gone too soon, never forgotten.

Darren sat on the pew, the hard polished wood like a paddle against his tailbone. It was impossible to not squiggle or find a position that was in any way comfortable. A hand, old with wrinkles and liver spots, veins painted just below the skin like a brook on a map, clasped his fingers and squeezed them together every time Darren tried to adjust himself – if it were even possible. Between his legs was his baseball, aged and tattered, but a comfort to him in this moment of dreaded sorrow. It was the talisman he had held onto the last time he sat on a pew, front row tickets to a viewing of immense emotional pain. The baseball had done nothing to quell his tears then, nor did it now. He grossly wept. His eyes swollen practically shut and surely bloodshot from days of grief. Snot oozed from his nostrils and ran like a wet slug over his lips. He wiped at it with the back of his suit sleeve, but it was like a faucet with a broken handle. There was no way to shut it off. Even with Darren's grandfather's arm around his shoulder and his grandmother's hand clutching his fingers, nothing assured him that everything would be alright. Nothing would ever be *alright* again, not with his mother inside that ornately decorated box with garlands of fresh flowers, her lying here on full display for the participants of the service inside God's hall.

Darren was to go first, be the first of all the patrons in the church to walk up the three steps where his mother's casket lay. Her body was ravaged and unrecognizable from the year of cancer treatments to end up here, in the coffin with an application of so much putty and makeup looking like human skin pulled taut over the sticks which made up a scarecrow.

"Try to sleep," his grandmother said with a kiss on his forehead. As if he could. Darren wasn't sure if he would ever be able to sleep again.

He rubbed the kiss off his forehead as if it had been left there like a smudge of dirt. It was a compulsion he wasn't even aware of until his eyes stung at the edges with tears and his throat hitched a bit. It wasn't like he hadn't cried before. Darren had cried plenty of times. Skinned knees, finger slammed in the car door, stepping on a mud-wasps nest, all things a boy would cry about. But if he cried now, just like he did back at the church, it would make all of this real.

Slumber did come by the waning moon as soft hues of blue touched the comforter; and as the minutes passed, the light rose until it illuminated the armoire. It was a soft light, only this one wasn't made by the man on the moon. Instead, it was coming from inside of the armoire, tracing the cracks between the hinges and the small gap between the closed twin doors.

Darren's eyes blinked. Then opened. Not because of the light across the upper half of his comforter where it had swept through the minutes of the night, nor the light behind him, growing brighter than the moonlight. It was a hum. The humming of a woman's voice. A song. A lullaby. One that Darren knew well.

He rolled over; and as his eyes fell on the armoire, the light blinked away. Darren rubbed his eyes, unsure of what he saw, the moonlight still a wide ray of warm light encompassing the shadows that ran away to corners of the room. Sitting up in bed now, Darren glanced at the armoire and rubbed at his eyes with the back of his arm.

Just my imagination, Darren thought. He laid back down and promised himself, just as before, that he would no longer sleep. This time he kept his promise. His eyes remained open until the sun traded light with the moon.

Darren's feet touched the floor, cool for the summer. The AC had run all night. His toes pulled the slippers to him, and his feet slid inside. He tugged on his t-shirt, which had ridden up his stomach, and cautiously approached the armoire. Darren's hand reached out steadily toward the double knobs, one screwed tightly into each of the twin doors. Darren huffed and pulled one of the doors open.

There was a shadow of darkness where the light couldn't touch because of the door blocking its path. There was no light bulb inside the armoire. That would just be silly. But Darren sort of wished it wasn't as silly as he thought it might be, even one of those bulbs that dangles and needs to be switched on by pulling a chain that always seems to be twirling from the bulb's socket.

Darren pulled the door open as fast as he could and stepped back as though he was going to be scalded with boiling water, but there was nothing there. Although, that wasn't exactly true. Inside were his clothes, hung up neatly. There was a ball glove and a bat that was propped from corner to corner behind his clothes. The glove held a tattered old ball with stitching that was almost completely worn away. In his mother's room there would be another glove, one that fit her hand, no longer needed. Darren squinched his nose trying to stave off the tears and bit his lower lip to focus. He didn't want to think about the other glove, or the times at the park when they would throw the ball from the mound to first base before the imaginary runner could get there safely. All the boy things his mother used to do because there wasn't and never had been, a father.

Everything looked normal. Darren reached out, almost balancing on one leg as he stretched. He tipped over his fingers and nudged the bottom of the bat until it came forward. Darren grabbed it just in time. He pulled away from the armoire holding the bat like he was at the plate. Only it wasn't a ball he was getting ready to hit, it was whatever lurked behind his clothes.

Darren used the metal bat to slide the clothes. The hangers screeched against the metal bar as they drew along it like fingers on a chalkboard.

Empty.

Darren looked at the wooden back of the armoire. The only darkness behind his clothes was the dark stain of the wood. No menacing shadowbat or monster lurking where the light could not touch. Darren stood in the beam of the sun ray, dust mites fluttering around his face like miniscule fireflies.

He huffed, screwing his face. Darren felt disappointed. Afraid, yes, but disappointed, let down that nothing had been there for him to strike with his bat.

"Breakfast!" His grandmother called from the kitchen, the scent of bacon now filling his nostrils. Darren tossed his bat into the armoire and slammed one door closed. He reached to slam the other when a square of woolen fabric fell at his feet. Darren bent over and picked it up. He held it so the garment opened, and Darren stared at one of his mother's "December-sweaters" as she called them. He looked up to the shelf above the hanging clothes, the one his mother used to harbor her colder season sweaters, packed tightly together like sardines in a can. Darren hadn't needed the shelf, so his mother had swept in and made the space her own.

Darren had forgotten about that. He was so used to seeing the sweaters that they had just become part of the scene in his armoire. He never gave it much thought. Although, he reminded himself when he started to have sleepovers that he'd have to move them, hide them somewhere, so the other boys wouldn't see the girly clothes in his room.

"Darren. Breakfast."

"C'mon." Darren shut the other door after he threw the sweater haphazardly into the armoire. As the echo of the rattling wood faded, Darren heard a thump. Soft. He knew it was another sweater. He hung his head. He would have to drag his desk chair over and put the sweaters back.

His mother's sweaters.

Sweaters she would never wear again.

He didn't hate them or even not like them. The two of them were just wrinkly and smelled like the ladies' section near the perfume at Macy's where all the other old people shopped. *Is that what they do all day when I'm at school?* Darren thought. The idea alone gave him a shiver. All those old people with their yellow teeth and discolored eyes, wrinkled faces, and arm flaps that looked like the pink wiggly skin hanging down from a turkey's beak. A gobbler? Was that what it was called? It didn't matter. He knew what it looked like.

"Gross," he whispered.

Darren didn't feel like doing his homework. How could the teacher even expect that much from him? Sure, it had been almost a week since they put his mother's – no it wasn't his mother in that box – the body in the ground. He was back at school after what the school counselor called a "grieving period." Darren just wanted to be left alone. He didn't need his homeroom teacher to give him a pitiful look, or the other teachers, even the janitor who'd never said a word to him, not even yelled at him when he got mud on the clean floor, looking down at him with a sorrowful glance and telling him "I'm so sorry for your loss." "Pfff," Darren grumbled. He didn't need it from the teachers, and he didn't need his friends looking at him and each other and everyone being so, so, so... quiet around him, like he was going to break down and cry like a girl.

I'm not a girl.

Remembering the day was fueling him with anger, and he threw his backpack on the bed and turned around, wound up, and kicked the dresser door of the armoire.

Ouch!

Darren turned and lifted his foot to see if he was bleeding through his sock. The stab of pain that jolted through his body made him think he must have at least taken a whole toenail off. He was about to curse under his breath when he heard a thud. It was from the armoire.

"Damnit!" The swear came out of his mouth without thought, and his eyes flicked to the door and then drooped down. The pain in his toe didn't hurt so much now. There would be no repercussion for his cuss. No extra tree of broccoli to begrudgingly digest for supper. No consequence at all. He could cuss all he wanted now, and somehow the thought of that made him never want to cuss again.

What was the whole point?

He didn't want to get his homework done, as if he was ever going to use long division in his life. Darren grabbed his backpack by the shoulder strap and dragged it over the bed before tossing it onto his desk.

Thud.

Darren turned toward the noise.

Laying where Darren had tossed it, forgetting – he didn't – to put it back on his mom's shelf, was the green sweater, the December-sweater. Again, he huffed. He was always huffing these days. Unmotivated to do anything. Ignoring his friends, hiding from his grandparents, faking stomach aches so his grandparents would believe he was sick – they didn't – before church. Everything seemed to make him huff these days. Couldn't he just be left alone?

Like that would ever happen.

Grabbing the desk chair, Darren dragged it on its two back feet across his small room. He put it to the side as he opened the armoire doors and then pushed the chair between them with a *thwack*! He grabbed the sweater, not bothering to fold it – it wasn't like she'd be wearing it – and climbed onto the chair. He could just barely see over the precipice of the shelf. A line of sweaters, most cotton or wool, he could never tell the difference, and tried to stuff the December-sweater up with the other ones. He pushed and shoved, but without it being folded there was no room for it to fit.

Frustrated, Darren huffed again and put one foot on the headrest of the chair. He tried to balance himself up high enough so he could push things around and make the sweater fit. Why wouldn't it fit? Couldn't he just be done with this part? He thought of his mother, lingering in his room, the laundry basket at the edge of his bed with unfolded clothes while he played Xbox, and her talking over the game no matter how high Darren turned the volume. She had a laugh in her voice, and he knew she was doing it just to annoy him. Secretly he wanted to laugh too but he was too old to play these kinds of silly games with his mom. He wasn't in kindergarten anymore. Not even second grade.

"Just. Fit." Darren shoved harder.

Clank –

Darren paused. What was that sound? He pushed the pile of sweaters he was trying to move backward again and – *clank* – the sound again.

"What the heck?" Darren reached up and tried to push the sweaters aside. When he couldn't do that, he pulled them down one row at a time. Frantically he got as many as he could out. Whatever had made the sound when he moved things around hadn't made a noise again. Darren was too short to see up on the shelf and even shorter to reach up there all the way to the back. He tried to think. Was there a ladder in the house? No. But there might be one in the shed. Only…how would he get it passed his grandparents?

A moment later, as quiet as he could, Darren dragged his desk across the room. It wasn't any taller than the chair, but he had a great idea. Darren got the desk against the armoire and put the chair on top of it. Sure, this wasn't the best idea, but it was all he had. He climbed the precarious structure until he could see inside the cavity between the shelf and the curved top of the armoire. It was darker than any other part of his room as though the armoire was some kind of gateway to another dimension that ate the light and anything that came near it. Like his hand, that was already reaching.

Reaching.

Reaching.

Reaching – his fingers touched something. It was cold and metal. Kinda. It didn't feel like metal, not like the railing on the bus or the legs of his school desk. This felt softer, if that was possible, and there was something on it. He couldn't be sure what, but it had divots and smooth rounded sections. If only he were an inch taller, he could reach –

There was that rush in his stomach. The kind you can only get from a rollercoaster, and Darren had it as the chair slipped and the desk moved on the slick wood floor. He came crashing down between all of it in a ginormous clap of sound like a hammer coming down on an anvil. It happened just as he knew it would.

"Are you okay?" his grandmother called.

"What in the hell," his grandfather said as they both came rushing in. "What are you doing?"

"Uh, just trying to get a sweater down. Couldn't reach it," Darren said.

His grandfather put his hands up to his forehead, clearly not enjoying going through this part of parenting at seventy-two, and said, "Darren, it's the end of May. Why do you need a blazing sweater?"

"Grandma keeps the AC up pretty high," he deflected.

"Ruth, turn it down," his grandfather said. "Darren, stop whatever you are doing and get your homework done."

"Yes, sir."

On their way out of his room, not closing the door behind them, he heard his grandfather say, "I'm too old for this, Ruth. Too damn old."

Darren turned so he was sitting cross legged and held the object from the back of the armoire in his hand. It wasn't quite silver, just like it wasn't quite metal. He held an ornate music box. There were carvings on the side like a carousel with small cherubs in between looking down at the horses as if ready to pluck them up to heaven.

"So you're what's been making all this noise."

As if answering him, the music box split in half, a circular door opening in both directions to reveal a dancer in the center of the carousal. The horses – even a lion –circled the inside of the small doors so that she looked like the pole holding the whole thing together. Darren searched for the small crank to make the music; but as hard as he tried and all the places he thought might open to a small compartment of gears to make the music box play, there was nothing.

Maybe it was just a fancy trinket.

His mother's fancy trinket.

After everything was put back the way it was meant to be, the trinket standing on his nightstand next to his X-Men comics and water cup – he was often thirsty in the night – Darren sat at his desk and opened his long division book.

His breath caught in his throat; and he spun around, without knowing where to look, his eyes falling on the trinket that sat motionless, his palms sweaty. A few beads of sweat formed along his hairline. His heart was racing so fast he thought he'd set off one of those monitor thingy's at the doctor's office.

Wings like the –

– from the nectar

Hummingbird

– those tired eyes

Just his imagination. That was all it was. He must have taken a bump on the head. It was just his imagination… imagination. Because it couldn't be – there was no way – it was impossible. He certainly hadn't heard bits and pieces of a –

Lullaby.

Darren avoided sleep at all costs.

He got home from school, his eyes bloodshot and swollen. He'd struggling to not let them flicker closed during class. He sat with the trinket. Its doors closed to the woman inside, the dancer at the heart of the carousel. He played with the doors, trying the latch to open them. It was sealed shut. Darren tried again. And again. Harder than he should have, but he was getting so frustrated that part of him just wanted to take the thing and throw it against the wall.

Huffing – like usual – he pushed himself along the floor with his sneakers until his back was against the mattress, his unmade bedsheets twisting over the side like a waterfall of fabric. Darren slammed the back of his head against the mattress in frustration. Nothing was working as it should have. First, he couldn't find the crank to wind up the music, and then it played on its own – he thought – and now the doors had closed, and the dancer inside had just vanished. And then there was the – well, he wasn't going to think about that. *That* certainly **had not** happened. Darren sure as heck wasn't going to give *that* any thought.

Who would believe him? Not that he was going to tell anybody. His friends would call him 'girly' if they knew he was playing with a music box. But if he slipped up, if he accidently told someone, like Dawn Ferrara, the most beautiful girl in school – way out of his league –if he accidently told her, maybe she would understand.

What was he even thinking? He couldn't go around telling people about a music box he was playing with! Not even Dawn Ferrara. Afterall, she didn't even know he was alive, even though they had sat in the same row since first grade. Alphabetic last names and all.

Darren reached and put the music box on his nightstand, climbed into bed, and turned on his Xbox. He'd downloaded a mature game his mother never would have let him buy. She would have taken his Xbox away for a month if not forever had she found him playing this game. Darren had even felt a little guilty about downloading it, but then he remembered it was his mother who left him. She'd left *him* all alone in the world. Stuck with two mothball smelling old folks who watched ME TV and fell asleep – snoring – by sunset. They were like wrinkly old wood-gnomes.

"Gross," Darren said. He pulled the sheets over him and played the game, trying to stay awake, until the controller slid out of his palms and his head rested on his shoulder and sleep took hold at last.

Darren stuttered awake. He had just nodded off. It hadn't been that long. He was sure of it. He could still keep his promise to himself. The game was still running, but his character was dead, waiting to be revived. See, he couldn't have been asleep for that long.

His head hung low when he looked out the window, the thin curtain half closed, while a moon beam illuminated half his body. The sun hadn't even been setting when he had turned on the game. Darren reluctantly gave in and reached for his remote–

It was open!

She was there.

The doors of the carousel music box had opened, and the dancer – still as a mouse – was there. He could see her. It hadn't been some kind of hallucination after all. How had it opened? Darren quickly grabbed the remote and shut off the TV. He went to touch the music box, to pick it up and examine it. Only his hands froze just a hair's breath away from the trinket. What if by touching it he would make the doors close again forever? He couldn't risk that. They were open though. He knew it. He knew he wasn't going mad.

Darren pulled the covers up to his chin, his room's only light was that from the evening moon; and he watched the woman inside. Her face pink, she wore a floral dress that was frozen in a swaying motion as she must have once danced around the music box. He could see the circular indentation around her. The way it should have moved, making her dance. If only the crank and gears would work. He couldn't find them. If he got brave enough, he would have to try again. There had to be a compartment, like a trap door, stowing the secrets inside.

It took only minutes of staring before Darren's eyes fluttered one last time and his eye lids drooped closed. As they did, the moon beam moved to reflect the worn glass of the music box, and the dancer glided in a circle, the music box humming.

A lullaby.

"You're eating fast," his grandmother said.

"You got somewhere to be?" His grandfather asked with a suspicious stare. The man, no longer looking formidable as he had in his early years – Darren had seen pictures – his voice still held a challenging baritone.

"Just tired," Darren said. He was looking down at his bowl of shepherd's pie while he shoveled as much as he could into his mouth, hardly taking breaths in between and barely taking the time to swallow a mouthful of milk. He *did* have someplace to be.

"Homework comes first," his grandfather said.

"Yes, sir." Darren finished the last of his shepherd's pie, not even bothering to scoop up the rest of the gravy with his piece of bread. He had always done that with his mother. "May I be excused?"

"Of course, honey," his grandmother said. Unlike his grandfather, she had a warmth to her smile.

"Thank you." Darren bounded up the stairs and shut the door behind him. He threw his backpack on the bed, not caring about his homework, no teacher pressuring him at school – the dead mom grieving period worked well. He just let it all pile up in his binder.

As Darren expected, the music box was closed.

He ran to the window, pulled the blinds, and closed his curtains. He knew, for whatever reason – power of deduction, supposedly – that the music box only opened at night. For the last week it had only opened at night. But each day when he came home, he wished it would be open. Darren wanted to hear the lullaby: the one his mother sang to him when he was little when she would hold him and they swayed like a boat on a quiet ocean in the rocking chair. She would hum to him the lullaby.

Hummingbird.

Hummingbird.

Hummingbird.

She would sing. He had always thought she made the lullaby for him. His mother had called him her little hummingbird when he was little because of the way he hummed when he was trying to learn how to speak. She would laugh, and it made him giggle. Darren was surprised he remembered these details. He thought the further away from his mother's death, the more he'd forget all about these minute details; but they seemed to become more pronounced instead.

His eyes wondered over to the music box, and he wished right now that it would open and sing to him. Darren could imagine his mother dancing alone, as she sometimes did to her old record player and its 60's poppy songs that made her smile bright and playful. Darren wished he had danced with her when she'd asked. But he was a big boy. And big boys don't go around "cuttin' a rug" with their mothers, as she'd called it while shimmying over to him and planting unwanted kisses on his forehead and cheeks.

Darren wiped at his eyes, climbed into bed even though the sun was still up, and hoped the music box would sing him awake. Remembering all these thoughts of how he hadn't been a good son, not dancing with his mother and avoiding her loving kisses. The only kisses he let her have were when her body had given up and her breath had smelt like a fish tank in need of a deep clean.

I'm sorry, mom, Darren pressed his eye lids shut as tightly as possible; but, like a small hole in a water balloon, the salty tears found a way through.

Synchronized, the doors of the music box opened as Darren's eye lids began to twitter and sleep was once again upon him. The music hummed and played its tune, the one that coincided with the lullaby. Only this time something new and unexpected happened. The gears turned beneath the floor of the circular dance floor and the woman inside the music box moved with them. There was a pole that protruded from her ceramic foot; and as the music box played, she spun – not fast – and rose up and down like a floating ballerina. Her dress looked as though it were actually floating around her body as she "cut a rug" all alone inside the glass enclosure. She made three rotations before the gears paused and her painted eyes and blushed cheeks looked upon a sleeping Darren.

> Hummingbird, hummingbird
> close those sleepy eyes –
> let my love take you away
> To the dreamland in which
> you will play –

The sound of the humming lullaby woke Darren. He saw her. Their eyes met, hers painted in a glow that would remain forever open, and his eyes blinking away the remnants of sleep. The lullaby played. This time it was no longer hidden when he wasn't paying attention, or just giving him glimpses of the sound. Darren watched the dancer slowly move. He sat up in awe and stared. This was unbelievable he thought. The dancer moved around. The pole made her rise and fall, her dress spinning as they twirled. The lullaby sang from the music box. Darren cocked his head and followed the dancer's every move.

It couldn't be possible. Just a coincidence was all. He was tired and sad and lonely. That was the reason he was seeing the unbelievable. Certainly, the woman danced inside an antique music box in need of a good polishing. He jerked his head and leaned forward.

"Mom?"

The dancer stopped.

The ceramic eyes blinked.

The lips, drawn on and painted with rouge, smiled. Her eyes looked sad, the way he saw his own eyes in the mirror when he woke in the morning and realized he was alone, that his mother was gone, buried in a manicured lawn with headstones, some leaning or sinking into the earth. The dancer moved again, her eyes closed now but her smile wide. Her arms turned, palms up as the song slowed; and she stopped, the gears no longer turning. Once more she faced Darren, but her hands looked as though they were reaching out, wanting to hold the hands of another dancer. It was the way his mother had held hers toward him when he had been too cool to dance with her.

Darren reached forward. He held the music box in his hands.

The lullaby played, not just portions of it but the whole lullaby with the words and humming of the tune that used to put Darren to sleep. He remembered, often asleep but on that precipice of wakefulness and dreamland, when he felt her kiss on his forehead to say goodnight while she whispered parts of the lullaby to him. It was the same thing he had done while sitting next to her in the hospital bed, the monitors bleeping, the oxygen tank hissing, his mother's lungs taking in shallow, pausing breaths as though the next breath might be her last. Darren had hummed to her as he had watched her dwindle from the liveliness of herself away to the barren vessel that had harbored her soul until her final breath was released.

In that moment, Darren reached to the dancer, the music box growing around him. He held hands with the dancer as they twirled around inside the music box. There were no more tears, no more sadness. He held her hands, his own now ceramic, painted peach, his pj's still on. The two swung around in circles, rising and falling like the animals on a carousel, horses of varying colors. They danced while the lullaby played, immersing them in the song. The doors of the music box closed and sealed, but inside the music box the two continued to dance.

Until the end of time.

12. Five Months Today
By Marinda K Dennis

It's been five months today,
Five long months since you took your smile away.
Your doggy in the window howls out in pain.
The brother you left is silent, nonverbal again.

It's been five months today,
And I fight back the tears.
Five long months rips away the years
We had with you and your electric blue eyes.

It's been five months today
Since you decided to leave.
Those left behind still hide pain as they grieve.
Your grace, your love, your creativity, just gone.

It's been five months today
And I still think you're coming home…
After practice, after school, after a meet, after a walk alone.
"You're just out of sight," my mind lies to console.

But no, it's been five months today.
A constrictor wraps around my heart.
It writhes and compresses as I gaze at your art.
Your steady hand, once creative and wild,
Now rests peaceful in a snow covered field so tender and mild.

13. Leaving Early
By Julia Gordon-Bramer

Troy embodied the second half of the nineties, if an era could be personified. Bill Clinton was our president in a sex scandal, the stock market was booming, technology began creating a new world online, and grunge music had destroyed mainstream pop with a growl called Nirvana. We looked for problems when there weren't any, like Y2K. We were on the edge of everything.

And there was Troy: hip, in retro amber-lensed rectangular sunglasses, sporting a long, braided goatee (often dyed blue, yellow, or green), and usually outfitted in 1960s and 70s bowling attire. His obsession with sound, fierce ambition, and calculated coolness fed the musical genius behind Sacred Nine, an alternative-industrial band in which my then-boyfriend, now-husband, Tom, played lead guitar. In Sacred Nine, Troy's production magic followed the melodic heavy sullen vibe of bands like Garbage and the post-punk weirdness of The The.

In a musical world of twenty-somethings, we were in our thirties, still young; but we didn't think so. Young enough that

95

we overlooked our blessings and forgot to treasure our limited time with each other. Still young enough to abuse our bodies and take our looks for granted. We believed in immortality, and while we knew intellectually that everyone's time was finite, everyone was not us. Others left by moving away, falling out of touch, or exiting the planet through disease, accident, or aging. We surrendered to our different dreams of music: mine, running a music magazine; theirs, to be in a successful band. And Troy was a leader in the scene.

"Arrive late, leave early," Troy said, arriving to concerts after they started or showing up to parties at 10:30 pm. "Let them miss you." He felt the same way about his band's performances, never wanting to perform more than once a season and staying onstage for under an hour to leave the audience hungry for more. He was funny, intelligent, and knew the bands we should listen to way before the radio found them.

Troy's wife, Eliza, was the lead singer, a shrewd businesswoman, and my best girlfriend back then. She wore heavy makeup and sported an androgynous, dark-rooted pixie haircut bleached white. With her heroin-chic figure, Eliza typically wore a black leather miniskirt and go-go boots everywhere, making her instantly recognizable as being in a band even if one did not know which band. And most *did* know because Sacred Nine had made it. Or just about. They signed onto Universal Records' Radioactive label, released a few records, toured America, and played in amphitheaters to thousands of people. They enjoyed photo shoots, bizarre clothing, fancy dinners with A&R reps, and per diem accounts. Although these expenses, they later realized, came out of their own pockets. It was hard work, and to make it in music one needs a kind of discipline not found in many rock stars. But the members of Sacred Nine, more or less, had it. My magazine, *Night Times*, featured them on the cover of our Christmas 1995 issue. The band had just nabbed the opening slot on a national tour with My Life With The Thrill Kill Kult.

They were praised in *Rolling Stone* and offered movie soundtracks. Their manager was the wife of one of the members of Black Sabbath, and their producer had worked with all of their musical idols. Sacred Nine was becoming famous.

Then, something shifted. By the late 1990s, the music world's power centers were redefined. Napster was how people got their music, and pirated digital singles dominated. The record industry all but collapsed, dropping bands and closing their smaller subsidiaries. Our city of St. Louis changed, too: the legendary Mississippi Nights, where Sacred Nine used to sell out, and other live music venues on the Landing were shuttered and then mowed over to make way for a new casino. The punk rock, DIY vibe of nearby Washington Avenue was also gentrified; and the dark windowed, dirty little clubs in hundred-year-old buildings with questionable floor strength that sustained sold-out crowds for Radiohead, Blur, and Stabbing Westward disappeared. The whole magnificent scene was killed by something called Progress. Tom and I moved in together. All that, plus band politics, broke up Sacred Nine. It's a long story, and not the one that I am telling here.

I ran into Eliza and Troy at The Galaxy, just as I had made the difficult, painful decision to take *Night Times* out of print. It had been my passion, and it was the sole thing that defined me for years. Aside from divorcing my first husband, which I'd done right before I started *Night Times*, it was the hardest thing I'd ever had to do. I'd rather they heard it from me.

Eliza hugged me in consolation.

"Sorry to hear that," Troy said, looking toward the empty stage as the Galaxy filled with showgoers. I knew then that Troy held a lot of anger toward me. That he had blamed me, in part, for Tom leaving his band. It got even worse shortly after, with screaming matches over the phone about some truth I'd leaked to the press. Once, he composed a long letter to Tom with various reasons that Tom and I should break up. I could see then that music for Troy, maybe for all of us back then, was the whole identity. But for Troy especially, if he was not musically successful, he belonged nowhere and was no one at all. Troy had to be everything or else he did not see that he existed.

Tom and I married, and we grew distant from Eliza and Troy but watched always with interest if their names came up in the paper or on the radio. Eliza and Troy's entire relationship depended upon the band; and with that gone, it seemed they could not endure. Eliza followed a secret passion, singing country music. And Troy? Troy ran too hard, too fast, as always, holding the same enthusiasm for drugs as he always had for his music. He formed a new band and did some production. But Troy let go of the reins of his life when the drugs ran off with him. He sold all of his new band's equipment without their knowledge. The story I heard was that someone found Troy in his apartment naked in the fetal position and called his family up in Fort Wayne to get him. He was promptly checked into a facility to clean up. Eliza reunited with Troy to help him, and because she loved him.

Nearly two decades went by. My kids grew up and left home. I dabbled in the corporate world before returning to school for my Master's degree in writing. I did a long stint teaching, and somehow ended up as a full-time professional tarot card reader. Tom and I occasionally reached out to both Eliza and Troy. After so much time apart, sins were easily forgiven. We had all grown up and owned our part in the madness. And Troy emailed back! He was trying to keep clean and still dicked around with music. He was interested in rocking out in the basement with Tom and reading my memoir, *Night Times*, about that 1990s era when St. Louis was an alternative music mecca, and Sacred Nine was on the top.

A few months later, Troy swung through town, reached out, and asked if we wanted to visit. We were excited to see him. If only Eliza could be there too. It would have felt complete. Troy explained that Eliza could not come back; reliving St. Louis and the people of her past was too hard on her.

Along with their old drummer Jimmy, we met Troy in a restaurant. Weight had always been an issue for Troy; and while he kept in shape in his rock star days, it did not come easily as he never had any kind of balance or moderation. Troy had gained probably 200 pounds. He was nearly as wide as he was tall. Once we were past the shock of his new body, it was a great visit. I tried not to judge as he ordered beer after beer, downing five for every one Tom and Jimmy had. Troy clearly was not doing well physically but seemed happy enough.

The guys decided to all jam together in our basement the next night. I ordered Thai food and hung out on the periphery, watching, giving them space to talk. Troy had always been the party guy; not just fun, but the *most* fun. Tom told me later that Troy said he'd been fighting addiction problems for decades. Judging from Troy's obesity, food was one of them. He told the guys he'd juggled sex, drugs, and alcohol all while they were on tour in the 90s. When the rest of the band went to dinner, Troy saw hookers or dealers. But now, he was trying hard to be a better person. He was even going to church.

Normalcy was a steep, unending, boulder field for Troy to navigate; and he never quite got there. He drank a lot of beer and smoked medically-prescribed marijuana at our home to get him through each day—and that jam session with the guys. He said it kept him strong enough to avoid the hard stuff. Anyone could see he was still an addict, still in a perpetual limbo of feeling something else beyond himself. It was heartbreaking but also easy to let it go as we enjoyed the talent that remained, that ear that knew perfect pitch, the brain that so easily intuited the right musical arrangement, even if in a fog. Our prodigal friend had come back, and we welcomed him. We loved him, and we always would.

Troy returned home to Indiana, and a few more years went

by. Then, in January of 2020, we received the hard news: Troy had died by suicide. We were all deeply saddened; but, somehow, not all that surprised. He had died by hanging. There were a lot of deaths that year and just before in music. I wondered to myself if they all wanted to check out before the stress of Covid. It was a lot for the strongest and healthiest of us to endure.

With Jimmy, Sacred Nine's former drummer, we drove the long haul to our friend's funeral in Fort Wayne in a January snowstorm with Tom reclined the whole time and healing from a recent knee surgery.

"I felt like when he came down to see us, it was to say goodbye," Tom said.

At the funeral, we reunited with Eliza and met Troy's family. The circle was complete. It was as good of a trip as any funeral can be.

A few days later, back home, I took a yoga class at a nearby studio. I still wasn't right. The gloom of my friend's loss hung over everything. I asked God for a sign that he was at peace on the other side, at peace in a way he could never be in this world. My instructor, Jenny, was not the usual one for that time slot. She impressed me with her ability to learn everyone's first names and use them throughout the class. We went through our hour of asanas, poses, and meditations, closing with our savasana and a blessing. As we sat with legs crossed, eyes closed, Jenny named each one of us: "It was a gift to share this space with you today, Sharon, Vince, John, Sylvia, Robert, Jane, Julia… and to Troy, who left early…"

"*And to Troy, who left early…*" It echoed in my head. I was stunned almost to tears. Yes, Troy chose to leave early. That's all. I had my sign.

14. It Came in the Mail Today
By Linda Holmes

It came in the mail today, that subtle little reminder of the day we spent together, just the two of us. It was a beautiful spring day with a gentle rain, the kind of day you pray for when you have something special planned. Trees and flowers were in that early bloom when you can smell everything growing, and new life is everywhere you look. People were rushing around us, but we really didn't pay them any mind. This was our time together, our day.

I hate to shop. Shopping has never been my "thing." I go in the store with a purpose. I'm one of those in, out, done kind of people. I am also a penny pinching, sales finding, coupon using terror. But this day was going to be different. This day was not about my schedule, my penchant for saving, my "get 'er done" timing. This was about someone special, my granddaughter.

We were really just getting to know each other, odd since she was already fifteen. She had moved clear across the country when she was young, and so our visits were few and far between. Ten years, forever in grandparent time. The occasional trips back were for a few days and always had to be shared with visiting everybody in the family, no real time to bond with anyone in a meaningful way. Trying to get caught up was like a chore at times, people attempting to cram so much into such short spaces of time. Tensions were high and nerves were frazzled, not a good bonding experience. There is a lesson there somewhere, I'm sure.

There was that trip after the accident that killed her father and gravely injured her brother, what a harrowing visit. The flight in from down south, the funeral, the constant telephone calls to check on her brother and Mom, staying in a home with a Grandpa and Grandma she had only seen as a small child, all the while worrying what was going to happen next. It was not exactly the visit you dream about. So many questions were swimming in her head, so many nightmare scenarios playing on her frazzled nerves. Then she was sent back home, clear across the country again into a world of worry and stress about her brother and the aftermath of the accident. She was trying to find a new normal while everyone else was strained. She was being tossed around like a beach ball. It was a rough time for such a young soul.

After a couple more years, it was a fast and wild move back home with all of us under the same roof Grandpa, Grandma, Mom, and the two siblings. Yeah, those were fun times! It's hard to live under the same roof when there are three generations involved. The constant trial of not stepping on toes or correcting the grandchildren made for a *lot* of tension for Grandpa and Grandma. It wasn't any more pleasant for Mom and the children having to live under Grandpa and Grandma's rules, trying not to rock the boat. It would have been different, could have been different… maybe not.

The clock moved again; the family moved again. But this time things were moving on in a good way; at least, it seemed to be that way from the outside looking in. The family was now only an hour and a half away from us. That was doable. We were finally getting the opportunity to do the "grandparent thing." We went to track meets and wrestling meets, sitting on those awful, hard bleachers, killing our backside, eating hotdogs and popcorn and yelling ourselves hoarse. It's a grandparent thing, and it was *awesome*!

This day was another milestone, shopping day. Not just any shopping day, prom shopping day. Prom is like a rite of passage. It is when you start to realize the little kid you picked up off the ground is no longer the little kid and that kisses on knees don't help like they used to. Prom was right around the corner, and my granddaughter had asked her Mom if Grandma could take her prom dress shopping.

Remember who her Grandma is? Well, how can you say no to a request like that? Of course Grandma was going to take this opportunity. My senses were just going to have to be in-sensed for a day. This was an honor that could not be missed.

The day arrived, and we were off to the stores. We naturally went to the secondhand stores first and found nothing impressive. There was a consignment shop in the old town area, so off we drove. We found some really nice dresses, although try to find a size nothing dress in a regular store, much less a consignment shop. We happened upon a couple of dresses and bought them, but they weren't the "wow" factor dress you want for prom, especially a first prom. They were more like homecoming dresses. There is a difference. You could see a little disappointment in her eyes, so what was I supposed to do? Grandmas do hate to disappoint the grandchildren. As much as I dreaded the obvious, we knew where we had to go.

"Let's check out the department store in the mall. They might have something nice." *I'm already three stores into my least favorite activity, and I am suggesting this venture? I hate department stores!* We had two dresses that would work, I was off the hook for this shopping thing. The rain was coming down a little harder, soaking us clean to the bone. *What was I thinking!?* I was thinking I wanted my little granddaughter to have the time of her life. I wanted this to be something beyond special. I wanted her to remember this for the rest of her life. I wanted to see her smile so big that she would outshine the sun. That was the memory I wanted.

So we got back in the car and were off to the mall and the detestable department store. We walked in and saw a whole lot of… nothing. Finding a store clerk on the floor was like pulling a chicken's teeth. When we finally got the attention of a floor person, we received that look. You know, the one you get when you are wearing your work jeans, a t-shirt, and ratty tennis shoes with your hair up in a ponytail, and you walk into the Ritz? Yeah, that's the look. The floor person with the "are you kidding me" attitude directed us to the furthest corner of this football field size store and left as fast as possible in the other direction. I know they get paid hourly, but really?

We stumbled into the correct area, two small racks of fancy dresses that I wouldn't put my dog in, that is if I ever dressed my dog. We were not impressed. "Well, we're here. We might as well see what this looks like on you. Sometimes the hanger doesn't do it justice." *Who is talking, and why are they doing this, and who are they trying to kid?* On the way to the dressing room, we saw it. This was the dress, and we both knew it. It was a beautiful midnight blue spaghetti strap with little silver sparkles shimmering all over. The fairy godmother couldn't have dreamed up a better dress.

You have not lived until you have seen the disappointed face of a fifteen-year-old completely transform into shear ecstasy. You have also not seen anything like a fifteen-year-old in army boots and a $200.00 midnight blue, better- than-Cinderella dress in the middle of a fancy department store. She was beyond beautiful; she was gorgeous! Her smile covered her whole body from the top of her head to her combat boot covered toes. This was her dress. After modeling it and beaming in delight, she redressed in her jeans and carefully laid her treasure into the cart. That should have been the end of it.

"Do you have shoes to wear with that?" some stranger's voice came out of my mouth.

"Oh, I can order online Grandma."

Hello! I was just supposed to get the dress, right? Grandmas can't do things halfway when it comes to special occasions. I mean, really, do you think that is going to happen on this granny's watch? I don't think so. We pushed the cart with her to die for dress clear across the football field of a store to the shoe department.

The shoe department was small enough that you had to wonder if they had anything that would be good enough to fit with the perfection of the dress. It took a little doing, but we found this strappy little pair of sandals in silver that sparkled when she walked in them. I looked at the price tag. They were on sale after all. I had to pick my jaw up off the floor, $80.00 on sale. *They were a few straps and a base for crying out loud!* I balked at paying over $20.00 for a new pair of sneakers! *Who in their right mind would pay so much for this silly little pair of shoes?* Of course, Grandma got them. After all, they were perfect. At this point I know some alien had taken over my brain. There was no other explanation I could come up with at that point.

We started to the front of the store to check out. "Mom is going to move the money to my account." She said as she dialed the cell phone. There was a little bit of a line, so we figured the money transfer had gone through. "Your card is declined for lack of funds," stated the girl from behind the counter.

Are you kidding me?! All right, Grandma's got this, we just won't eat for a few days. Grandpa will understand. It's all good.

The peanut gallery behind the register says, "You know we have a special if you get our credit card today..."

So much for no credit cards, of course I signed up. I guess it was a discount, we got the dress and the shoes for less than the dress alone would have cost. This penny-pinching Grandma was feeling pretty good. My little Cinderella was beaming. Who was I kidding? She made Cinderella look like a grubby little street urchin in that gown.

You would think we were done: got the dress, got the shoes. No more shopping! No. Nope. All done. "Do you have a bra you can wear with that?" It's that same strange voice. I thought I had been possessed at this point.

"I can get one online Grandma."

"Do you know what size you wear?" *Are grandmas supposed to ask these questions of their grandchildren? Why am I prolonging this shopping trip? Who hijacked my senses?* Her grin answered my unspoken questions. We piled our treasures into the Jeep and headed for the other side of the mall. We were on a mission.

You thought the grubby granny going into the department store got strange looks. Now this old white-haired grandma was taking her sweet little fifteen-year-old granddaughter into the "naughty shop" at the mall. Not only that, but granny was asking for a fitting for the bra, "if you please." As you know, there is no good reason for wasting time if you have to be in a store. Of course, I had to peruse through the new stock to see if there was anything in the lingerie that would be of interest. Grandpa is old, not dead. After a few remarks about how difficult or not it would be to get in and out of the silky arrays, I decided against buying any of them… for now. I wouldn't want to embarrass my granddaughter in the middle of the store.

With the bra purchase made, we left the store. We had been at this for several hours at this point. There was a gelato and candy store across the way, and it had been a long day, so we stopped in for a tasty treat before heading back to Grandpa and Grandma's. Also, Grandpa was out of sugar free candy. Any excuse for chocolate is a good one. Everyone needs a splurge every now and then.

When we got home, we had to send a picture of the completed ensemble to Mom, so into the bedroom walked my little granddaughter. A few minutes later out came my darling, grown-up Angel. Gone was the little girl who rode down the slide with me at the park, who couldn't wait for birthday cake, who splashed in the puddles on a rainy day. No sign of the terrified girl who waited for her Dad's flag draped coffin on the tarmac as she stood between the strangers who were her grandparents. No sign of the trauma that had been her brother's long recovery period when she had been the mother hen. Here was the glimpse of the beautiful young woman my Angel was meant to become. Poised and perfect, she beamed with joy.

Her smile lit the room as Grandpa gushed over how amazing she looked and took pictures to send to an anxious Mom on the other end of the instant messenger. It was a perfect day. Angel was going to the ball in style, and we were a part of it. The thought of the whole day and the wonderful outcome still makes me smile.

Now, Grandma's smile turns to tears. My Angel is gone. I don't understand why. We had just had a wonderful time at the zoo with her family and friend earlier in the week. We made it through the loss of her great grandmother and had started talking about all the things she had planned for the summer. She had a job, a boyfriend, a career in mind. She was looking into colleges that had the forensic science program she loved so much. Life was good.

And just like that, it was gone. She decided it was time to go without asking us if we were ready for her to go. Loss and confusion tainted her view. She lost sight of those of us who loved her, and she left us behind. She chose to leave. Why?

I miss her. It is two in the morning, and the tears run down my face. It isn't the first time; it won't be the last. But this time it all started from a little piece of mail that came today. The department store sent me a letter.

15. Heaven Born
By Marinda K Dennis

Heaven born starlings are the brightest souls to bless this earth.
They burn deep and strong and are gone much too soon.

~ For our dear Evangelina—our Angel on high—for my
Daddy who held her then and holds her again now, for her
protective pup Milo who runs by her side in the open fields of
heaven, for her best-friend and my dear GiGi—a fighter to the
end, and for my sweet Uncle David, who watches over us now
with his pipe in hand and his hat in place—the one item that
always goes home when Uncles David does. ~

I

"Please, just take her out! Please!" Day two of labor proved
to be more difficult than the entire eight months of pregnancy
leading up to this point.

The nurse took my clenched hand in hers. "Shhh!" She
patted the top of it. "Don't let *this* doctor hear you say that,
hon," she whispered. "You don't want that on top of
everything else." She rubbed along the ridging of the bones

that clearly showed due to the extensive weight loss from the complications of the pregnancy. "I'll see you through this night. I promise." Letting my hand go, she disappeared into the bathroom and reemerged with a damp cloth. "Here, darling." She dabbed my forehead. "Try to lay back and rest between contractions. I know it's hard, but try anyway."

I eased back onto the pillow and let my eyes close.

"There you go. Deep breaths when you can."

"We're both going to make it, right?" My eyes pleaded with hers.

"We will do everything we can." She wiped a tear from the edge of her eye and turned to check the monitors. "I have other patients I have to tend to, but I'll pop in as much as possible."

I nodded and hee-hee-ed through another intense wave of contractions.

"Good. Keep doing that." She gave my shoulder one last squeeze before she walked out of the room and down the hall to tend to women who were not at risk of dying or losing their unborn daughters that night.

I closed my eyes and breathed deeply, relaxing as much as my rock-hard belly would allow. In time, I drifted into a meditative state, not dreaming, but not entirely present in the moment either. It was somewhere in-between like the meditations I would take my Yoga students on before I could no longer teach classes due to the hyperemesis gravidarum that kept me close to the restroom or a puke bowl.

I started on the beach at sunset, a relaxing scene to be sure. I transported to sparkling ocean waters to swim alongside dolphins, fun and freedom that my current condition would never permit. Another contraction yanked me back to reality, back to now. The intensity would not allow the breathing to calm it. I laid heavily on the call button. The nurse rushed in. "It hurts" was all I could manage as my breath stalled in my throat.

"I can't give you another bolster. I'll have to call the anesthesiologist who placed the epidural." She pulled up her walkie and made the request.

For a moment my vision blacked out. I woke up to a cool cloth on my forehead and the taste of vomit in my mouth. "He's on the way. Hold on, Sweetie."

A man in a white coat whisked in. The night nurse Julie helped to lean me to one side for him to check the location. "It looks fine. Everything is good." He stood up and leaned against the railing of the bed. "We've already placed it twice. I'm not sure what else to do." Julie rolled me onto my back as another wave of pain hit.

I motioned with a finger for the anesthesiologist to come closer. He leaned in as if I was going to whisper. I gripped the collar of his coat and pulled him within an inch of my nose. "Is it morphine based?"

"What?" Confusion littered his face.

"The epidural. Is. It. Morphine based?" I paused at each word with a snarl in my voice.

"Y-yes" he stuttered, his deep brown eyes wide with fear.

"Morphine doesn't work for me," I spat out before having to hee-hee again. I released his collar to grab for Julie's hand.

The proclamation appeared to put him off balance as he stumbled backwards tripping over the wires on the floor that kept me hooked to the wall and life. "I'm sorry. I'm sorry. I didn't know. I'll fix it right away." He clamored out of the room and returned soon after with a new bag of medication to hang from the metal hooks over the bed.

Julie held my hand the whole time. The relief was not entire, but it was enough, and it was instant. Everything relaxed, at least partially, including the rock-solid abdominals.

I cried and allowed my head to lull to the side.

"Better?" she asked.

Words escaped me, and fatigue overtook me. All I could do was nod. She released my hand. I saw her check the monitors and frown before I drifted off once again. I settled somewhere between the land of the waking and the realm of dreams.

Clouds floated around white marble pillars so thickly that I couldn't see the ground beneath my feet. The stars sparkled above brighter and closer than anything I had experienced on earth. I could have sworn that had I reached out, I could have plucked one from the deep purple sky.

I turned slowly in place looking for anything familiar. Finding none I instinctively reached down for my belly. It was flat. My baby was gone. I panicked and gripped tight with both arms.

"Don't worry."

I jumped at the deep voice.

"She's right here." A tall, muscular man emerged from behind the pillars holding a little pink bundle.

I took a step back. His features were familiar, but I couldn't quite place them.

"I'm sorry it's taking so long." His strong bass voice echoed around the space even though he spoke softly. It resonated through my heart like something from years ago hidden just from my memory. "I couldn't bear to part with her just yet." He looked down at the bundle. "She's one amazing little girl with more spirit than even you had when you were younger."

The embodiment of his youth, he looked just like the picture I would tromp past up and down the stairs and smile at. I gasped. "Daddy?" It was barely a whisper. He was about 200 pounds lighter and had all his hair. There were no scars on his face from the skin grafts needed to battle the cancer, but the smile and the eyes were still the same. And the voice, it was the deepest I had ever known and would either cower at if in trouble or revel in when he cheered from the sidelines at track meets.

He nodded, never taking his electric blue eyes from the blanket in his hands.

"I know you are struggling down there right now. I know that this pregnancy has nearly claimed you both twice already." He continued to gently bounce the blanketed baby. "Just know that anything that causes this much tribulation is worth more than all the riches your world has to offer. She's going to be a handful, but she's also going to be magnificent. Her fierceness will touch a lot of lives."

I stayed cemented to one spot, unable to move, unable to force myself forward.

After what felt like a small eternity, Daddy took his brilliant blue eyes from the bundle. They drilled into me with a wave of love and strength. "She's yours now." He gave a single nod. "Take care of her."

I looked from Daddy to the baby he held and back again. "Is that really—" The words stalled in a choked effort to speak.

He nodded with a smile. "Take care of her."

I too smiled and cried. "I will, Daddy. I promise."

"Her BP is rising again. She can't take much more before she strokes." Julie rushed around the room prepping towels, blankets, and a tray of instruments.

"Ten. She's at a ten! Call for the doctor." Someone else ordered.

Dazed and confused, my head lopped from one side to the other in an attempt to regain my bearings.

Julie rushed to me and patted my hand. "It's alright, Hun. It's almost over."

A wave of pain punched through my gut and exploded out my back.

The doctor ran into the room with his sterile gown, mask, and a hair cover. He held his hands upward waiting. One of the nurses assisted him with his gloves. "Are we ready?" His eyes smiled as if this was a joyous occasion and not a life and death situation.

The room spun, and I puked up the little bits of melted ice chips I had been allowed to have over the last two days.

"We need to get that baby out before her heart gives out." Julie stood fiercely, her frizzy hair haloing her head.

The doctor looked at the monitors. The corners of his eyes dropped with the bottom of his mask. He took up his seat at the end of the bed and barked orders to those in the room.

Another nurse walked into the room and tapped Julie on the shoulder. "Shift change."

Julie glared the woman down. "I'm not going anywhere. I saw her through the last two nights of labor, and I'm not leaving until I see her through this." Julie turned and took me by the hand placing her other firmly on my shoulder. "I made a promise, and I intend to keep it."

The other woman stepped back slightly, looking for orders on what to do next. The doctor turned to her, "I think we're all covered in here, Nurse. Thank you."

She slunk out the door with her shoulders slightly drooped.

Pressure built to a momentous explosion. My heart beat loudly in my chest overpowering all sounds in the room. The doctor gave strict orders, and the nurses complied. At one point they handed him large metal spatulas.

Julie stayed at my side. She didn't use words, just motions. She did her best to keep my eyes on her. She hee-hee-ed and whooo-whooo-ed with a purposeful nod, getting me to fall in sync with her breathing.

When I thought I couldn't push or breath or exist any longer, the doctor set a slime covered baby girl on my belly. She looked up at me and gave a deep sigh as if to say "are we done yet?"

I touched her cheek gently as a tear ran down my own. A movement in the doorway caught my attention. Daddy stood there with a smile of pride on his face. He gave a single nod before turning as if to walk out into the hallway. His figure faded with each purposeful step he took.

I turned back to my newly born baby. "I will take care of you, my little heaven born Angel. I will keep my promise, Evangelina."

II

Nearly sixteen years later, the lights flickered overhead. Carmen sat next to me, strong, stoic, the woman I wished I could be in that moment. She barked orders for the nurse to get Sandy.

I sat next to her on the hard waiting room chair, numb, staring at the speckled patterns on the floor. My tears dried up and yet threatening anew. All I could think was *This can't be real.*

Sandy arrived, her own eyes glistened with fresh tears too. "Oh, Honey. I'm so sorry." She looked at Carmen and back at me.

"I didn't know if I could give her anything." Carmen looked to the nurse.

"I need you to get her this, now." Sandy scribbled something on her prescription pad and handed it to the ER nurse. "I'm her primary care provider. Go."

My Angel swings my hand as we walk to preschool. I try singing "Twinkle, Twinkle Little Star" with her. I get as far as "I wonder what you are" when she stops midstride practically yanking me over in the process.

"But Mommy, you can't wish on a star," she says.

"Really?" I respond. "And why not?"

Without hesitation she answers, "Because stars are just big balls of gas millions of miles away."

Sandy rubbed my knee. I looked up to see her kneeling in front of me. "I need you to take this." She handed me a small cup with a pill and a little glass of water to chase it down with. "It will take a little bit to hit, but it should help. I'll send a prescription to the pharmacy." She turned to Carmen. "Can you pick it up for her? I'll call it in so that I can explain the situation. They should let you if they know you're the one coming for it."

To me it was all words, noise, nonsense. I went back to staring at the floor.

"Jim, you made it." Carmen got up and pulled a chair over next to me. "Sit here."

I could hear the click, click of his cane against the cold, hard linoleum. He sat and took my hand. I pressed my lips together hard and looked up. His face mirrored the stoic look of his mother. I envied them both for their strength though I knew the reasons for it were something no one should have to have endured. He took me by the hand and held it firmly. Warmth spread up my arm, but not nearly enough to warm my frozen soul. He took my chin in his other hand. It was so big that it cupped my cheek and framed my face all on one side. His callused thumb rubbed up and down in a soothing motion while his other hand squeezed mine tightly. "No matter what. We'll get through this together."

I looked over to Carmen who had an arm around my frail looking son and back to Jim. My heart calmed. My shaking stopped. In that moment of truth, I knew that no matter what, our family would survive.

We waited for what seemed like hours. Sandy waited with us. She had her nurses reschedule her appointments for later in the day. Finally the ER nurse returned. She looked somber, and my heart sank. I bit my lip and stifled a cry.

"I'm sorry, Ms. Dennis. The doctors did all they could."

I wailed harder than I thought possible. An earthquake shattered my heart in two and threatened to bury my soul in an avalanche of pain.

"Do you want to say goodbye? We have her covered with a sheet. You can come in and see her if you want to."

I composed myself long enough to nod.

Sandy grabbed me by the arm to stop me and looked me directly in the eyes holding my full attention. "Before you do, you need to know that just like finding her, this is another image you will never be able to get out of your head. Are you ready for that?"

I nodded again. Jim hurried to my side while the ER nurse led the way. We walked through the waiting room door into the short hallway. I could see a closed door at the end. In that moment, the hallway extended into a never-ending tunnel. The smell of medicines, IV bags, antiseptics, and death drifted down through the empty space between us and that door. No matter how far I walked it was always just out of reach until finally the nurse opened the door, and there she was. My Angel. Her eyes were gently closed, she looked like she was asleep, but the lesion where the rope had dug in and the blood had pooled around it on her left side told me otherwise.

I sat on the edge of the bed and laid my head across her chest. "She's cold. My baby's cold," I whispered. I hugged her tight and wailed until I slipped into song like I would when she was little and ready for bed.

"Mommy, will you sing me another one?" her sweet blue eyes look up at me from behind blonde bangs.

"I've already sang you five songs. What is left to sing?"

She twists her lips to the side in hard concentration. "Silent Night. That one's my favorite."

"Silent night," I choked slightly trying to get enough breath to support the notes. Jim's hand went to my back and Sandy came around to the other side of the bed to place a hand on my shoulder. "Holy night." They both rubbed gently offering strength I needed for that moment. "All is calm. All is bright." Jim stepped in closer. "'Round yond Virgin, mother and child. Holy infant, so tender and mild." The words rang through the hollow room as my breath heaved heavily in my chest. The after tremors of the earthquake rumbled through me with each new pained note. "Sleep in heavenly peace. Sleep in heavenly peace." The last word lingered like a soft whisper lulling her into her eternal slumber.

Jim's hand gripped my arm and lifted me up. "Come on, Honey. It's time to go."

I nodded and looked down at her one last time as Jim and Sandy led me out of the room and back to the waiting area where Carmen sat with my only living child.

III

The funeral home had a day just for family. Our son was at summer camp in an attempt for continued normalcy. There would be time enough for him to face reality when he came home to the extreme quiet and emptiness, a hole where she should be but never would be again. Althea, our Angel's little Corgi, padded along the sidewalk from the parking lot to the door. Her little numb of a tail wagged excitedly. We had told her we were going to see her girl.

Angel sits on her father's lap screaming hard. Every dog we had introduced to her thus far had cowered in a corner, one even peed before running behind the adoption coordinator. "Don't you have any dogs left that might be a good fit?"

The woman squirms uncomfortable while Angel continues to scream a blood curdling infant scream that never stops, not even for breath. "There is one I could bring in, but he was severely abused. He could have some violent tendencies."

"Bring it," I order clenching a hand to one side of my head while Angel's father continues to bounce her in a desperate attempt to calm the nine-month-old babe.

"Come on, Honey," Jim pulled me from my thoughts. He nodded to the door he held open that Althea was pulling toward with all her thirty pounds of muscle would allow against the harness and leash.

I pressed my lips hard and swallowed. "Okay." We stepped in together with our excited fur baby, waiting to see our little girl in eternal slumber.

"Welcome. We have everything set for you." The funeral attendant lead us down the hallway to a solid oak door. I could hear the band Flogging Molly muffled from behind the door. We inched our way through and around another corner. A TV in the corner streamed images of my Angel, her life, her smile, her teen 'tude, her time with friends, her moments with family. Flogging Molly's "If I Ever Leave This World Alive" transitioned into the darker intonations of Disturbed's "The Sound of Silence," one of her favorite songs. There in the center along the far wall, my Angel rested silent and still. I picked up Althea while unhooking her leash so that she could see her girl even though we were still in the back of the room. The squirmy little dog whined in excitement and jumped out of my arms running for the wooden coffin. She jumped and yipped, begging to be picked up, begging to join her girl.

The adoption coordinator brings in the shaggiest, most raggedy dog in the entire shelter. His hair was long, curly, and wiry all at once though he has soft tufts along his chest. Angel continues to scream uncontrollably. Her father turns to me. "I'm not so sure about this one."

The dog looks up with large brown eyes. He gazes at the tiny wailing babe on her father's lap, then up to the father as if to ask, "May I?" before licking the rounded, red cheeks. The crying stops instantly. Angel stares at him stunned, then smiles with a little laugh. The shaggy black and white mutt turns his mishappened, masked head back to the man holding the child and gives a small tail wag almost asking, "Did I do good?"

I turn back to the adoption coordinator. "This is our dog. He's going home with us today."

"Come here, Brat Baby." Jim set his cane against the side of the coffin and lifted the little dog into his lap. "There's your girl." The little corgi heaved and tried to crawl in with her long lost human. She sniffed at the body and licked the arm. Her wagging stopped for a moment, and she whined harder. She nuzzled her head against her girl trying to rouse her from her deadly sleep. Jim placed the wiggly pup on the floor.

I stood there unable to speak or move just taking in the sight of my miracle baby, the one I nearly died to have. The black cloak her aunt made draped perfectly around her with only her hands and forearms showing. The Cladaugh ring was placed on her right hand that she might know of her heritage and the love we had for her, and the triple moon to match my own on her left. Her black dragon earing weaved around one ear, a Christmas present from Jim not six months before. Her red hair brushed across her face like a bird's feathered wing. Tears stung my eyes and splashed freely along the satin lining that held her comfortably as I placed the ashes of her first dog

Milo at her side.

"Is everything how you want it?" The attendant asked.

I wiped the tears away and took a few steadying deep breaths. "Grandma's ashes. I was told that she was going to be holding Grandma's ashes. Those two were thicker than thieves. She needs to be with her grandmother." Jim wrapped an arm around me and rubbed. I could hear an almost silent shhhhh. Althea jumped at my legs begging to be picked up like a toddler.

The woman shifted uncomfortably. "The ashes wouldn't fit in her hands.

I stood taller and squared my shoulders reaching one hand down to the little tricolored dog pawing at my knees. "They are getting buried together. Is there any way we can fit them in the casket together. Please?" The last word cracked splitting through a note from "The Sound of Silence."

Jim squeezed hard. "At her feet maybe?"

I nodded. "Yes, can we try that, please?"

The woman hurried out and returned with the bright red box that contained what was left of my grandmother, not even two months gone from this world, and likely the last loss that threw my daughter into a world of depression from which she couldn't escape except like this. I pressed my lips hard and clenched my teeth until I thought they might crack. The woman opened the bottom of the coffin to show the wrappings around my daughter's feet and legs, necessary due to the tissue and bone donation, a wish noted on her driver's permit as "Donor." She worked my daughter's feet apart just enough to place her great-grandmother with her.

"Boop." GiGi runs a brush of red paint over Angel's new shoes.

I watch my five-year-old's jaw drop. "You not apposed to do that."

GiGi looks surprised as though no one has ever told her "no" to anything before. "What?"

"I said, you not apposed to do that. These are my new shoes. You apposed to put the paint on the canvas. Like this." She grabs the brush from her best friend and dabs at the spot GiGi had just been working on. "See."

"Marinda, you have one of the most remarkable little girls here." Grandma smiles at me. *"Do you mind if I keep her for an hour or two today?"*

"Why not forever, GiGi?" her little voice rings out, *"You's my best friend. We going to be best friends for evers and evers."*

"How's that?" the woman asked showing me her progress.

"That'll do. They were meant to be together. I know that. They wouldn't want it any other way."

Althea jumped up one more time, attempting to claw her way into the casket. Jim held her up. I reached in and touched my daughter's face gently running a hand along her check before breaking into a strain of "Amazing Grace" against the Irish jig of Floggy Molly.

After I ended, Jim gently took me by the shoulders and led me out with the Corgi dragging behind, none of us really wanting to leave our girl again.

IV

I sat silently between Carmen and Jim and across from my oldest brother whom I hadn't seen since before my daughter was born. My oldest sister talked to me in a baby voice. I hated when she would go into that mode. I wasn't five and afraid of the dark anymore. I was a grieving mother, not an infant. All the same, I knew she was trying to help.

I dabbed at my eyes trying to keep a strong, stoic face for the flood of students who stood in line waiting to venture through and view the girl they had all come to call friend and to hug the mother who had given rides to early morning practices and provided donuts and games for long, out-of-town activity trips. The somber faces were both eager to express their sympathy and pained to have to do so.

I stayed where the line that wound out of the room, down the hallway, and to the main door, could reach me. Even the president of the college for which I had been teaching just over two years made his way through, respectfully dressed in a suit and tie. He expressed his deepest sympathies and said, "Anything you need, let me know," and he meant it. One of the benefits of working for a small establishment was that everyone pulled together like family during the trying times.

Eventually, the flood of students turned to an older crowd, family who had travelled in from out of town. More siblings with kids in tow, aunts and uncles, cousins I hadn't seen in what felt like ages. They all came to offer love and support.

Aunt Diane and my cousin Lisa inched their way forward. Aunt Diane wrapped me up in an embrace as well as her walker would allow, the aftermath of a car accident that nearly claimed her life at the start of the year. Lisa followed close behind. "Uncle David couldn't make it today, but he promises to be here for at least the graveside." I nodded and pressed my lips together hard. I hadn't seen any of this side of the family in years, not since before our move to Florida when Andrew was only a baby. That they would come after all this time sent me into fresh waves of tears that refused to be held back.

"Come on, Marinda, drink this." My older sister handed me a bottle of water. "You need to stay hydrated."

I shook my head no and pushed it aside. The crowd blurred together, and I sway slightly suddenly unsteady on my feet.

"At least put it with your purse for later."

"I'll make sure she drinks it." Carmen grabbed the water bottle and placed it on the floor just under my chair. "I'm pretty good with stubborn kids. I raised five of my own."

I gave a small smirk and squeezed Jim's hand. My lip quivered when he returned it with firm pressure of his own.

"Why don't you sit down, Honey?" his soft, deep voice resonated in my chest and broke something loose.

I obeyed him with a small nod not even paying attention to those in the line anymore.

"Marinda, I'm so sorry." Angel's Uncle Stan from her dad's side of the family kneeled in front of me and gave an awkward hug. He was the one man, the one person on that side of the family, that I knew I could count on. Even when the children's father had died, he'd been there with words of comfort and encouragement for the kids and me, unlike most of the rest of the family. I returned his hug and just held on for a while, feeling the warmth that attempted to pierce my heart but just couldn't. He let go and stood up.

His short wife moved in next to him. Even sitting, I was only a few inches shorter than she was. "Marinda, I just—"

My chest heaved for breath. I clawed at Carmen's arm. *Anyone but her!* my brain screamed. Jim helped me to my feet. "I need air. I can't breathe." The room swayed and tilted.

Everyone has gone home. It is just Jim and I sitting in the silent, empty house, too big for two. Andrew is with his Grandma Carmen, and Angel… It hasn't even been twelve hours, but it feels like an eternity has passed in that time. We sit just holding each other watching who knows what on TV to fill the void.

My phone rings. I see the caller ID. Their dad's parents. I can't handle that right now. I shake my head. Jim asks, "Do you want me to answer it?" I can't seem to find my voice, so I nod.

"Hello." His voice is steady. He's never had to deal with these people

before. He has no idea what to expect, but I do.

It's the mother, the matriarch who tyrannized my marriage and eventually put an end to it. Her falsely sweet voice is clear even though she's not on speaker phone. She wants to be heard, obeyed. "Is Marinda there?"

"I'm sorry but Marinda isn't available right now." Jim's still cool, collected. He knows how to navigate problem people.

"Oh, well, can you give her a message?" She doesn't even wait for him to answer. "Let her know that the plot next to Angel's father is still available. She is more than welcome to bury Evangelina out there."

"Thank you, but it's been taken care of." Jim's tone changes slightly. It's barely perceivable unless you know what you are listening for.

"Are you sure because she really should be buried with her father." Her curt tone cuts through me. Again, she doesn't wait for a response. "Well, just let her know."

"I will. Thank you." He hangs up making sure she can't say any more.

We go back to our show. After a while I say, "Thank you. I really didn't want to have to deal with her tonight."

Jim and Carmen steadied me and walked me out of the room. The walls spun out of control. I was almost certain that I was going to pass out before we could reach the doorway. I could hear my sister behind me trying to reassure Aunt Brenda that I was just overwhelmed, that it had been a long day, that there had already been so many mourners in to see me, and that I would be back just as soon as I was able.

Aunt Brenda's voice floated through the hallway. "I just don't understand." At the sound of it, my breath caught in my throat and whisked me back to that night once more.

Not twenty minutes after the first phone call my cell rings again. My ex-sister-in-law's name pops up on the caller ID. Again, I shake my head and bury it deep against Jim's side. "I can't deal with her either. It's just going to be a repeat of the last call."

"Do you want me to answer it?"

I nod.

"Hello." This time he's ready. His voice is firmer than it was for the last phone call.

"Is Marinda there?" I can hear the strain in my ex-sister-in-law's voice. I know that strain. It's the same tone she had used to practically accuse me of my ex-husband's death even though I was well over a thousand miles away and fully divorced from him by then. Almost the entire family had blamed me for him not talking to them because I had refused to take any of their calls anymore and had told him that he needed to be the one to talk to his own family, that I was tired of being the go between for people who despised me and treated me like shit. And because even he wouldn't talk to them, they assumed that I must have been the one to blame.

"She's not taking any calls right now."

"Oh, well, can you give her a message?" The voice on the other end is tight, insulted.

"Sure." His inflections note that he already knows where this is going.

"Can you tell her that Mom wants to offer the cemetery plot next to Angel's father? They really should be buried together. He was her dad after all."

"It's already been taken care of." A hint of strain and restraint creep into his voice.

"Well, if you could let Marinda know anyway. Angel really should be with family."

"I'll let her know." Jim hangs up the phone before the woman can utter another word. He sets down my cellphone. Before he clicks the movie back on, he looks at the phone almost as if waiting for it to ring again, or to spring forward and bite him like a snake.

Jim and Carmen finally managed to guide me out to the truck. The heat outside was a welcome feeling compared to the ice in my limbs and numbness in my heart. Jim lit up one of my cigars and handed it to me. My sister came out to check on me. She pointed across the parking lot. "The ones who were bothering you are leaving," her voice once again in that baby talk tone, but I didn't mind it as much this time.

I could hear Aunt Brenda from across the parking lot shouting, "But I don't know what I did. There's no reason for her to treat me like that."

"Just get in the car, Brenda," Uncle Stan was firm, but gentle.

The phone rings for a third time that night. I look at the caller ID and breathe a sigh of relief. Aunt Brenda's name shows through with a photo of her round smiling face, friendly, harmless, innocent. Jim reaches for it.

"It's okay. I can take this one. She's safe." I flip the phone icon up to answer. "Hello." My voice is small and timid. I'd been talking all day and feel like I just can't talk any more. The phone call for the tissue and bone donation had taken a full hour to get through. It was more than I could handle, more than any mother could handle, the permission of giving away pieces of your child to save someone else's.

"Hi, Marinda. It's Brenda." The resonance in her voice is not her usual caring, nurturing self. It's reminiscent of her sister's voice, of the woman who wanted her way no matter what.

"Yeah."

"Look my sister has been trying to get ahold of you."

I swallow hard. I don't like where this is going. This does not *feel safe.*

"She thinks you should bury Angel with her dad. It's a really nice cemetery and Uncle Stan and I have spots out there, so it's not like she won't be with family." She sounds irritated, as if I've insulted her or called her something profane.

I clench and unclench my jaw while chewing on my tongue to keep from saying something I know I'll regret later. "It's already taken care of. Thank you for calling." I hang up before she can say anything else.

Jim takes the phone gently from my hand and places it just out of my reach. He looks straight ahead with the remote in hand, but he doesn't push the play. "The next person who calls about that damned cemetery plot is going to have to deal with me, and they aren't going to like it." His jaw shakes slightly. I press tightly into him, companions in loss and grief.

Uncle Stan ushered his wife into the car. Aunt Brenda still threw unbelieving glances my way unable to understand what she had done to cause such a reaction. I finished my cigar and allowed my family to usher me back into the funeral home to be on display next to my deceased daughter for the other mourners to feel a connection, a closeness to the one lost.

V

The pastor stood tall and stooped over at the shoulders all at the same time behind my daughter's closed coffin. He lit the black candle for remembrance and signaled the procession of mourners to come forward. He did beautifully with the content I had sent to him. When he met with Jim and me a few days before to ask about what we wanted for the service, I had told him that I wanted something to help the teenagers who would be there and asked if I could write the service and send it. He had humbly agreed.

Now, in front of the crowd of mourners, he followed all of it flawlessly, showing his own heart in the process with choked back tears and seamless transitions from one segment to the next.

"As we close out, the family has one last song to share. Before we do, so that you understand the context, the family shares this song to honor their Irish heritage which celebrates a life when a loved one passes." He looked back down to his notes and read them exactly as outlined, exactly as he'd promised the bereaved parents. "While we mourn Angel today, the tradition of her forefathers is that of rejoicing in the life that Angel lived, the Irish Wake (nonalcohol based though). And live she did. She travelled to 28 of the 50 states. She did her first year of cross-country training on the side of Mount Washington, the highest peak on the Eastern seaboard. She canoed and sailed the Gulf of Mexico countless times. One sailing trip she even splayed herself across one of the hulls and threw her arms back like the mermaids you see on the fronts of old wooden ships."

"Mommy, look!" Angel's smile takes up her whole six-year-old face. "I'm a mermaid, Mommy!" The saltwater splashes her unexpectedly, and she sputters to get it out."

I laugh. "You are a beautiful Mermaid, my little Honeybee."

The pastor's voice cut through the image. "She loved tubing on Big Lake with her little brother and parents and going to summer camp. At one summer camp in New

Hampshire, the whole crew, counselors included, jumped from a bridge into the waters below. She was so excited that the first thing she told her mom when getting picked up from camp was 'Guess what? You know how you always ask if your friends jumped off a bridge would you do it to? Well, I did. Twice.'" He held up two fingers just like she had.

Angel grins from ear to ear, proud of herself for having tackled her fear of heights and still on a bit of an adrenaline high from having done so only half an hour before. She flatlines her lips and slides her head from side to side like a pop star before bursting out laughing.

"In Florida at her favorite beach, she had the chance to swim with manatees but thought what touched her was a shark and ran screaming from the waters. She wasn't afraid of some of the more unique creatures though. She held a baby alligator in her hands and, at one point, a large boa around her shoulders. She was always asking for a bat as a pet.

"Her travels with her Grandpa Monkey and Grandma Minion took her to Hawaii where she saw Pearl Harbor, one of her dad's favorite historical sites. There she swam with dolphins. At home, she scaled the side of a mountain, enjoyed rock-climbing walls with friends, sitting around the role-playing game tables with Andrew, Sammy, Matt, Seth, Joe, Bob, Petra, the Dark Phoenix crew, and so many more. She had even hoped to start up a game campaign with her friends here."

Matt pushes his glasses back up his nose on the edge of his seat. He rolls. His shoulders slump. "Nat one."

Joe points at him. "You are officially enslaved by the magic of the stone. You must help the followers with their cause."

Matt pounds at nothingness in the air, "Blood for stone!" he yells. "Blood for stone!"

A twelve-year-old Angel laughs so hard she falls out of her seat. She quickly rights herself looking around to see who noticed.

Joe points to her. "Just for that. Roll for sanity."

Angel rolls. She groans. "Five."

Joe smirks. "You fail. You, too, are now helping the followers of the stone."

She looks at Matt and shrugs with a half-smile before joining in on the fist pounds at nothingness. "Blood for stone!" She strikes a single hand straight up into the air with the rallying cry, "Blood for stone!"

The pastor's voice cut through each memory he pulled to the forefront of my mind. "For sleep overs, Angel would tell ghost stories trying to scare the others present, and she was always looking for the supernatural at every turn. She found her stride at Falls City High School as she participated in cross country, one-act, the high school haunted house, the first year of all girl's wrestling where she was voted as the rookie of the year by her team, speech competition, and track. And thanks to the upper classmen who counted her as friend, she had the opportunity to go to prom and after prom."

Huffing breaths could be heard from over half of the crowd present, some stifling cries of agony, presumably from the memories that were once joyful, now tainted with loss.

The pastor paused long enough to allow the youth to recollect themselves, a tender mercy from the pulpit before he continued. "Through all of this life experience, the truth is that she laughed deeply. Her smile could wrap you in a warm embrace of emotions that you didn't even know you needed in that moment. And when she hurt, you hurt with her. You don't know why. You just did. She was a force to be sure, and a smart one at that. At four years old on their way to preschool, she stopped mid-step on the sidewalk while her mother sang 'Twinkle, Twinkle Little Star' and proceeded to inform her mom that 'you can't wish on a star because it's a large ball of gas in the sky' and that was that."

The group of mourners laughed though whether out of memories of their own or because of the echoes of her personality that rested in those lines, one could not be entirely sure.

The pastor gave a slight laugh himself and a sorrowful smile. "Yes, you knew that if she had accepted you for who you were, you were loved unconditionally and fiercely. You don't know how you knew it; you just did. She was your mama bear when you needed her to be and your hug buddy when you wanted it most. She was the embodiment of love itself wrapped up in this beautiful blossoming young woman with a heart big enough to touch as many lives as she did in her short time on this earth. And on that note, we are going to listen to the final song 'Come and Get Your Love.' Her parents said that anytime this song came on, you could see her in the back seat, bopping away, even through her saddest moments." He gave a nod and the song resonated through the rafters and the crowd.

"Watch this," Jim nudges me as he fiddles with the iPod containing his playlists. He hits the button changing the song. The opening notes of "Come and Get Your Love" fills the truck.

I chance a glance in the rearview mirror. Angel's frowning face bops in time to the music, her reddish-brown hair flipping in front of her eyes.

Everyone in the front pews swayed in time to the music, some sang along. All had fresh tears running down their cheeks. I placed an arm around my son and drew him in close, and Jim did the same to me.

My sisters stood up from the pew behind us and danced their way to us from the aisle in true Irish Wake fashion. They kneeled in front of Andrew and took his hands getting him to dance in his seat and even smile and laugh.

Angel smiles from the back seat as she sings in time with the radio. Her arms flail as if she's playing the light saber music game on the virtual reality headset. The song comes to an end, and she looks up at me through the rearview mirror surprised that we are watching. "What?"

Jim and I both laugh. "Nothing," I say. "It's just good to see you so happy."

The notes closed out, and the sorrowful joy bled into the fresh pain. A cutting tone from the back commented on the inappropriateness of the service. I recognized my ex-mother-in-law's voice, seated in the very back by the ushers to avoid any conflict. My mom's doing to protect Jim, Andrew, and me from sharp tongues.

Let her criticize, I thought. *She can't hurt me anymore. Not after this.*

The pastor resumed his position and wiped away a tear of his own. "And now, the family will proceed Angel out on

'Silent Night.' Please join us for the singing of one of Angel's favorite hymns.

The music played, and the funeral director led the casket down the aisle and out of the sanctuary. I followed behind my daughter's coffin with Jim's arms around me, the only things keeping me from collapsing as I recalled that day in the hospital and singing the same song to her one last time. Just as my voice carried her soul onward, the voices present lifted me just enough to find my courage, if only for a moment.

VI

We stood on the gravel road looking inward at the open graveyard. The blue tent next the hearse marred the serene scene of knee-high corn that bordered three sides of the more than a century old sacred site. The ancient sycamore tree, well over forty feet high, stood in the corner, remained still and steadfast, a testament of the strength carried in its trunk and boughs. The old swing that someone had put in years ago dangled in the shadows of the noonday sun.

Jim shook the hand of a large man. "You must be Uncle David. She talks about that hat and pipe all the time."

Uncle David grinned, holding his pipe between his perfect teeth. "Does she?" He gripped the pipe in one hand taking the hat off with the other at the same time and somehow running three fingers through his short reddish grey hair, dulled from its once brilliant red that screamed of the Irish heritage that bore it.

Kathy, Angel's second mommy as she was often called, embraced me in a breath crushing hug. I buried my head in her shoulder to allow a few tears to escape before sucking the pain back inward. "I'm going to check on the other kids." She pursed her lips hard, obviously fighting to stay composed.

I nodded, giving her arm a squeeze before turning back to Jim and Uncle David. My favorite uncle wrapped me in a large bear hug taking me back to when I was little and he would dress up as Santa. Each child was given a present, a candy cane, and a gentle but firm bear hug that lifted you off your feet. While he didn't get my feet off the ground this time, the effect was still the same: warmth, comfort, love, peacefulness. It all faded the moment he released the embrace.

The funeral home director and his son, one of Angel's teammates from both cross country and track, inched in. "Shall we?" They motioned towards the blue tent with the hard chairs waiting.

Jim grabbed my arm on one side and Uncle David supported me on the other. My feet refused to move. The men had to grab my hands tightly, and both leaned heavily on their own canes as they led me forward. Every muscle tensed and ordered me to run in the other direction. I choked and cried before the wails erupted, "I don't want to be here. I don't want to be here. Being here makes it real. Please, I don't want to be here."

A hand from behind placed itself on my shoulder followed by another on the other side. Two more hands, two more people to help move me forward. They squeezed my shoulders almost in unison. Together, the five of us proceed toward the tent. I happened a glance down at a headstone, Kenneth Eugene Dennis.

"Honeybee," I call. "Where are you hiding?" I stand up from where I had been stooped next to my Daddy's grave marker. I walk toward the large marker for the Dennis family plot area. I creep softly, slowly, before jumping around it yelling, "Gotcha!"

From the fields along the back, I hear a soft giggle.

"Come on, Angel," her father scolds. "Your mother called you. It's time to go."

"She just playing," I counter. "Let her be a kid."

He holds our son Andrew by the hands, helping him walk. He huffs and turns toward the car, making his way in baby steps to accommodate the nearly one-year-old boy.

I stroll around the tree where I find Angel with her back flat against the trunk holding a hand over her mouth to stifle more fits of giggles.

"What are you doing, my silly little Honeybee?" I kneel down next to her.

"Playing with Poppop and Granpa." She ran around to the board swing hung from strong ropes in the old sycamore tree.

I dug my heals in looking at my Daddy's grave, the man who married a single mother and adopted her four little girls when he didn't have to, the man who had raised me and been there for every hurt and heartache during my youth. "No." I tried to back up, but the many hands would not let me. "No. I don't want to be here. Being here makes it real," I screamed. The sound rolled up and down the hills of farmland, settling in the streams that crawled through the area.

The hands pressed me onward. I allowed my feet to stumble forward. The group inched towards the tent. The funeral director led the pall bearers, six of her friends and two uncles, with the casket under the tent to her final resting place.

Angel swings "high to the sky" as she calls it.

"Do you want me to push you?" I step closer hoping she'll need my help this time, want my help.

"No. I a big girl. I swing."

"Oh, okay." I step back and sit on the ground just watching her. "Are you about ready, Sweetie?" I glance over to the car. Her father is already belting her brother into his car seat.

"No." She puts her feet down to stop and wraps her arms around the ropes in protest with her bottom lip puckered outward.

"What's wrong, Honeybee?"

"I wanna stay here." She kicks at the dirt.

"Here?" I regard the antient cemetery with the 150-year-old headstones and the beautiful blue sky. "Why here?"

"Cause Poppop and Granpa here."

The pall bearers situated the coffin carefully on the taunt straps over the freshly dug hole, and the hands led me further into the tent. I lost all willpower and turned to Jim, clutching at him, grasping him tight and crying over his shoulder, "I don't want to be here. This can't be real. Please. I don't want this to be real." I sobbed hard burying my face in his shoulder while other hands squeezed my own from behind.

Jim embraced me, encompassing my whole being and hurt inside of his own for that one moment. "I know, Sweetie. I know," his voice ripe with pain. We stood there, two parents grieving together at their daughter's graveside service. The world vanished, and it was just us for that eternal minute of solitude and anguish. My cries subsided, and Jim reluctantly released the unionized entwining of our suffering. "They're waiting for us." He put a hand under my chin and lifted my face to meet his eyes. "It's time to put her to rest, Honey."

I nodded to him and allowed the sea of hands to carry me to the front row seats.

The pastor's wife held a silver goblet with a Tree of Life on the front to match the marble vault with the same tree on its top. The pastor held the three stranded silver cord my mother had woven together from two different cords found at the craft store, a grandmother's tribute to her lost granddaughter. He introduced it as my daughter's cord of life and shared the scripture about the strength of the three cords and how together they are not easily broken. The air sat heavily, oppressive and unmoving.

I turned my head to the old sycamore tree with the swing where she used to play. It swayed slightly somehow without a breeze.

"But if you stay here, I'd miss you too much, Honeybee," I tell her.

She stands and leans heavily on one rope thinking. "Okay, but Granpa says I can come back any time, and Poppop says I can always come play with them. Can we, Mommy? Please?" Her big blue eyes like a China doll's grow even bigger with the irises taking up almost all of the space, and her hands, clasped together, come up under her chin.

"You'll have to take that up with your dad. We have to move to Florida. I'm not sure when we'll make it back up."

Her hands drop, as do her eyes.

"But when we do, I promise that we'll come back to visit."

Her whole face lights up with a smile that reaches from one ear to the other.

I sat numbly staring at the coffin. My mom got up in front of the crowd. "We have balloons for the youth to release in memory of Angel. Those who would like to participate, please join us at the back of the tent." She made her way to where my siblings stood with plastic bags full of butterfly and unicorn balloons. All the youth present, even Andrew, joined in the reverent moment just like he had at the bay with his sister to remember their dad.

After a moment of silence in which we all watched the glittering wings of the butterflies and prominent pink horns framed in rainbow manes float out of sight, the funeral home director cleared his throat to draw the attention back inside the tent. He held up a coin from off the top of the marble vault. He explained that this was to signify the tree of life and serve as a reminder of the dearly departed. He gave one to each of the family sitting in the chairs before inviting the rest there to come up for a coin from the vault.

While everyone moved forward, I snuck out the side of the tent to the small black gift bag we had brought and someone had seen fit to leave for me by a tent pole. I grabbed out the Monster drink and moved to where GiGi's headstone stood waiting for the end-of-life dates to be added from her passing earlier that year. *They got their wish. They will always be together.* Angel's headstone would be situated at the foot of the grave while GiGi's already marked the head. I placed a hand to the precious stones and shells she had placed there herself in the fresh cement after Poppop had died when I was about the age Angel was. "GiGi, she loved you so much that she just could not be without you," I whispered. "Take care of her for me, like you did when she was little."

I turned to the crowd while still kneeling at the headstone. Using my best teacher voice to call the group to attention, I popped the top on the can and held the Monster high. "We are Irish, and at an Irish funeral you pour one out for the dearly departed." I stifled a choked sob before continuing, "Angel wasn't old enough to drink; so today, we pour out her favorite energy drink." I tipped the can and allowed the green fluids to quench the thirsty earth. I emptied it fully, shaking the can for good measure before getting to my feet once more. "For Angel!" I held the can high to a loud and enthusiastic response of "For Angel!" from everyone present. "If you want to pour one out for our Angel, please feel free to do so."

Others stepped forward with their own cans of Monster ready to honor their fallen friend.

I found Jim at the back of the tent talking to Uncle David. I hugged Jim tightly and buried my head against his. Something rumpled the top of my long, blonde braid. I reached up to feel the wool tweed of Uncle David's hat. I turned to him with fresh tears in my eyes.

"Why don't you hold onto that for now?" he said.

I pulled it down and clutched it close to my chest before

lifting it to my face and taking in the scent of fresh pipe tobacco, just like when I was a kid. It filled my nostrils.

"I told him to blow a few extra puffs in there for you so that the smell would linger." Jim hugged me from the side. "I remember you telling me you had good memories from the smell of the pipe smoke."

I nodded and placed the coveted treasure back on my head knowing that someday it would be called home; because when Uncle David goes home, the hat goes home too.

VII

A little over two months later I held the tweed wool with the letter folded neatly inside close to my heart, clenching it tightly. Aunt Diane stood in front of me, the fresh look of loss painted her pained face. "Uncle David told me at my daughter's graveside that I could hold onto this for now." Tears streamed down both of our faces. "Everyone knows that when Uncle David goes home, the hat goes home. That's the rule." I held it out to her. "I have to follow the rule." I cried hard. "Uncle David's been called home, so I brought his hat to be home too."

We both sobbed and Aunt Diane pulled me in close for a tight embrace. Tears ran down our cheeks, the most recent in a series of too many losses. She pulled back and gently pushed the offered token back to my heart. "No, Honey. He wanted you to have that. You need to keep it."

I cried all the harder. "Okay," was all I could muster up.

Even Lisa, Heather, and James, my cousins, insisted that their dad had wanted me to have that piece of comfort and to keep it.

I pulled the letter out of it and handed the paper to Aunt Diane. "At least take the letter, please." I looked deeply at her. "I can't do much, but writing I can do. Will you at least read it and know why I offered? Please."

She sobbed anew. "I will." She took the paper and held it to her own heart. In that moment we were not aunt and niece but sisters in a painful summer of loss and sorrow.

The organ started up, our cue to find the seats at the front for the family. I sat with Jim. Andrew was squished between us wrapped in hugs. This was the fourth funeral for our family since GiGi had died four months ago. Too many losses. It wasn't good for a child to know this much pain this early on. He wasn't even twelve yet, and this would be the fifth death in the family since his father had died. Jim placed a hand on the boy's lap as if reading my mind while I wrapped an arm around Andrew's slender shoulders. Together we mourned in silence in support of the family who had lost the biggest piece of their life: a husband, a father, a grandfather, a man who only knew how to spread love to others.

Halfway through the memorial service, the choir sang backup to the soloist. Her soprano voice displayed her professionally trained operatic skills. I played with the green lace pull over, the same one I had worn for Angel's graveside service. I reached up to my head covered by the hat Uncle David had given me that day. *When Uncle David goes home, the hat goes home,* I reminded myself. The table in front held his pipe and pictures of the jolly face that had brought so much joy to those around it.

The soloist finished her robust rendition of the traditional hymn selected by the family. The pastors, three of them, all associates of Aunt Diane's, stood at the front ready to pass out the communion of bread and wine. They invited the congregation to join with them in singing "Amazing Grace" and to come forward to partake.

Being part of the family, we were only three rows back. The ushers stood next to the pew and motioned for those who wished to participate to proceed to the front. Only Andrew and I stood. The rest in our row remained steadfast in their seats.

We inched our way forward, and I sang with the organ and those still sitting with hymnals in hand. When I was little, this had been my Daddy's favorite song to sing at church; I had memorized it early in my life, listening to his deep bass voice that would reverberate off the church walls.

I paused for a moment straining my ears. There were only four people between me and the front where you took the small plastic cup of red wine and a piece of the bread extended in offering by the pastor. Was that a bass voice I heard in the rafters? It was rich, full, and deep just like Daddy's had always been. A tear slid down. I wiped it away and continued singing. *It's my imagination,* I told myself.

The bass voice remained rich and strong and was joined by a mellow baritone that was full of life with a slight hint of Irish lilt even though it had belonged to someone born in the states. They were unmistakable and high above the crowd of mourners. The two voices danced together in melody and pace along the rafters, up and down, and low but there. Another tear glistened on my cheek. I squeezed my eyes shut, willing myself to stop before I was overcome to the point of the ugly cries of pain which sat rooted in my chest from all the losses suffered over the years.

A tentative soprano joined them, a young voice trying to find her footing among the other two. It was her voice, my Honeybee's, my Angel's. I kept singing to prevent myself from falling to my knees. The tears flowed steadily down my cheek as I took the bitter cup offered me. I drank the wine, and I ate the bread. The trio kept up with the congregation and at times seemed to lead them though no one else took notice or found it to be out of the ordinary. The song ended long before the mourners had all received their communion offering, each exchanging a heavy heart of sorrow for the promise of Christ's love.

Before finding my seat again, I looked to the front, and there they were, Daddy, Uncle David, and my Angel at the altar together. The two large men stood strong on either side of the young girl. They all three looked at me, gave a little nod, and slowly faded from sight.

I made my way back to the seat I had vacated, back into Jim's arms. No one else appeared to have noticed the three voices that had joined us or the figures at the altar and their disappearance. I leaned into Jim and cried quietly into his shoulder for a moment at the realization that this heavenly vision was mine and mine alone. This visitation was both a message and a promise that my little Honeybee was safely guarded by two of the men whom I loved the most during their time on this earth and that she would be under their care in the halls of our ancestors, just as the legends of old promise the heavyhearted and bereaved.

About the Authors

T Antoff

T Antoff is a historian, writer, and artist whose home will always be in Scotland. Never without a pen and notebook, writing has been a constant companion their entire life. They currently live in northern New Hampshire with their partner, two dear friends and housemates, three black cats, and a loving rescue pug.

Marymartha Bell

Marymartha Bell is a dangerous person to love, having outlived two husbands before she met Bobby Bell. A semi-vegetarian, she married a cattleman. Both she and Bobby did a little bit of a lot of things. She loves education, has a BA degree, worked as a technical writer in defense and aerospace, a biographer and editor, taught preschool, was a behavior therapist with autistic children, elementary and high school students. The only thing she did for long was mothering and boasts four adult sons who are self-reliant, loving individuals. She currently lives in the east with her goofy dog.

Christina Chilelli

Christina Chilelli is an avid creative writer who primarily focuses on historical fiction and historical fantasy pieces. They are a graduate of Tiffin University's Master's in Humanities Creative Writing program, and currently a doctoral student in Murray State University's Doctorate of Art in English Pedagogy program. They tend to focus their studies on the importance of diverse and accessible literature and feature strong women and Queer characters in their work. The piece "Little Ghost" was written after the passing of their childhood dog, Napoleon, as a means of memorializing and dealing with their grief.

Marinda K Dennis

Marinda K. Dennis is a short story author, novelist, and poet. She holds an MA in English and an MFA in writing. Marinda teaches college composition, appreciation of literature, and creative writing at various locations across the United States. In addition to this she edits works for other published authors and enjoys time with her husband Jim and their son Andrew.

Sara Fowles

Sara Fowles grew up in New Hampshire, where the ever-changing seasons taught her to appreciate rather than fear the signposts of change. She loves corgis, coffee, and her husband, in no particular order. Her previous work has been published by Crooked Cat and Great Old Ones Publishing. You can visit her on Instagram @sarafowlesfiction and find her dog-related adventures on TikTok @dogpuppyandme.

Christopher Frost

Christopher Frost is the author of *396* as well as the novellas, *Last Exit* and *The Door at the Top of the Stairs*. He has had many short stories published in *Down in the Dirt* magazine as well as *The Ethereal Gazette*. Christopher is an advocate for mental health awareness, because of his own struggles, and participates in many charities including the annual Run for Suicide Awareness 5K. He lives in New Hampshire with his wife and three daughters.

Julia Gordon-Bramer

Julia Gordon-Bramer is a poet, occasional professor, Sylvia Plath scholar, and professional tarot card reader. She is the author of *Fixed Stars Govern a Life: Decoding Sylvia Plath* (Stephen F. Austin State U Press, 2014) and the *Decoding Sylvia Plath* series (Magi Press, 2017). In 2023, her books *Tarot Life Lessons* (Destiny Books) and *The Magician's Girl: The History and Mysticism of Sylvia Plath and Ted Hughes* (Inner Traditions) will be released. She lives in St. Louis with her husband, Tom Bramer.

Linda Holmes

Retired paraprofessional, accountant, and caregiver, I currently live with my husband and his service dog. My favorite thing is spending time with and caring for family.

Ellen Meister

Ellen Meister is the author of eight critically acclaimed novels, which have been called, "powerful, moving and emotional," as well as "hilarious and poignant" and "heartbreakingly funny." Her books include TAKE MY HUSBAND, THE ROOFTOP PARTY, and LOVE SOLD SEPARATELY from MIRA/HarperCollins, and THE OTHER LIFE , DOROTHY PARKER DRANK HERE, and FAREWELL, DOROTHY PARKER from Putnam/Penguin. Her essays have appeared in Publishers Weekly, Wall Street Journal blog, Huffington Post, Daily Beast, Long Island Woman Magazine, Writer's Digest and more. Ellen is also an editor, book coach, creative writing instructor, and screenwriter.

Quantre Moore

Quantre Moore is a college freshman born and raised in Kansas City, KS by a single mother alongside six siblings.

Gregory Norris

Gregory L. Norris writes for short fiction anthologies, magazines, novels, and the occasional episode for TV and film. He lives in Xanadu, a grand old house in New Hampshire's North Country which his late husband Bruce restored in 2013. Writing, he often says, is the heartbeat within his heart.

Loriane Parker

Loriane Parker writes fantasy fiction and is a graduate of the 2011 Odyssey Writers Workshop. Her publications include her short stories "Thief of Souls" in *Thunder on the Battlefield, Volume I: Sword* and "The Orb of Shadows" in the anthology *In the Shadow of the Mountain.* A fan of Manga and Dungeons and Dragons, she lives with her two Welsh Corgis near a wildlife preserve where bald eagles soar overhead and wolves howl in a nearby Sanctuary. To find out more about Loriane and her writing, visit her website at www.lorianeparker.com.

David Singer

New Hampshire resident, rapidly approaching the Age of Curmudgeon, not to be confused with the Age of Aquarius, David is an ex-surfer boy from So Cal, author of the Classanr Series of western novels, ex-movie maker and general cut-up who humors himself making web pages and stacking wood for winter. A systems analyst at heart, and as all good editors should do, David can find fault in just about anything when he puts his mind to it. Fortunately, he offers probable paths of mitigating opportunities, thus preventing himself from being totally insufferable.

Made in the USA
Monee, IL
25 February 2023